GET
SOME
LOVE

GET SOME LOVE

Nina Foxx

AVON BOOKS
An Imprint of HarperCollins*Publishers*

HarperCollins books may be purchased for education, business, or sales promotional use. For information please write: Special Markets Department, HarperCollins Publishers Inc., 10 East 53rd Street, New York, NY 10022.

FIRST EDITION

Designed by Elizabeth M. Glover

Library of Congress Cataloging-in-Publication Data

Foxx, Nina.
   Get some love / Nina Foxx.
     p. cm.
  ISBN 0-06-052648-3 (alk. paper)
 1. African American women—Fiction. 2. Inheritance and succession—Fiction.
 3. Grandfathers—Fiction. I. Title.

PS3556.O98G47 2003
813'.54—dc21

2003048517

03 04 05 06 07 JT/RRD 10 9 8 7 6 5 4 3 2 1

For my girls,
Sydney, Kai and Brandie.

In memory of
Brison Hamilton and Elvie Powell.
Thank you.

Acknowledgments

If my friends didn't do or say the things they do, I would have no kernels that give birth to ideas. Thankfully, I have lots of warm people around me who are funny even when they don't mean to be.

Thanks to Robert Scott, my brother, for giving that stuff he keeps in the freezer to my non-drinking friend, Kwame Alexander. Kwame, for teasing (after drinking it) enough for me to utter, "Can a sister get some love?" Thanks to both of them for helping me flesh out the beginnings of this story.

The numerous friends and family who read and re-read drafts without complaints (that I could hear): Jill Hubley and Pam Lipp—yes, I am convinced that some people would just wait. Barry Jennings—thanks for the chocolates that give me brain fuel. BTW, I'm running low. Lynda Scott—thanks for being my best friend and convincing me that I could do anything. I love you. Brandie Scott—you are the best sister-niece I could possibly have. Shia Barnett; my sister, Stephanie Bratton; Charlenne Greer—thanks for the truth and encouragement.

Thanks to those who offered endless encouragement, even when I refused to "do lunch." Michele Davidson, Sharon Radovich, and Kim Greyer. Maybe just a quick cup of coffee, okay?

Those friends, old and new, who encouraged, advised and supported, even if you didn't know you were doing it: Evelyn Palfrey, Lolita Files, Eric Jerome Dickey, Victor

Acknowledgments

McGlothin, Victoria Christopher Murray, Matt Johnson, Tracey Price Thompson, Guichard Cadet, Prolific Network, Peter Arnel (CBS Radio Networks) and Keith Sage-el (Inner City Broadcasting).

Those ladies at Master Martial Arts and Master Um, for giving me a place to let out my frustrations and work out the kinks. (Kam sa ham ni da!) Sorry about the bruises.

My fabulous editors, Carrie Feron and Gena Pearson, for nurturing. My agent, Elaine Koster—thanks for making things happen and guiding me.

The numerous book clubs and bookstores that supported me: the phenomenal sister at Large Book Club in Milwaukee, The Ivy Readers of San Antonio, The Good Book Club and Pam Walker Williams, the Capitol City Good Book Club (Austin), the Texas Writers' League, Emma Rodgers at Black Images in Dallas, the Pettis' at Jokae's in Dallas, The Black Library Bookstore, the Keltons' at Our Story Books in New Jersey, the stores that make up the St. Louis Black Booksellers Association, and the wonderful independent booksellers who work so hard to get the word out there every day.

My sorors of Alpha Kappa Alpha Sorority, Incorporated, who support me endlessly, without question, in the spirit of sisterhood.

Last, but not least, my husband and my daughters, for letting me have a room of my own and not caring if it looks a mess. (I really do have a special kind of filing system.) It would not be possible without any one of you.

October 2002

1

Just when you think you have it under control, life has a way of throwing major curveballs. Angelica thought about the turn her life had taken in just a few hours and blinked back the tears that obscured her vision. She was racing along Interstate 10 toward home. The last exit sign she remembered was for Orange, Texas. Two days. A lifetime. So much had changed. A few days ago, when she left Baton Rouge to visit her friend in Bessemer, Alabama, Pop-pop was just fine, doing what he did every day. He was in the office at the funeral parlor, preparing to embalm his latest newly deceased client. Angelica had been there with him.

"This is an art, baby girl, you know that?"

"Ugh. You've told me before, Pop-pop, I know." She had crinkled up her nose at the thought and smell of the embalming fluid.

"It's a special time. Folks should look their best so they can go on properly."

"Whatever, Pop-pop." She'd waved her hand in the air in a gesture of dismissal. He always seemed sentimental when he talked about his job. It was kind of morbid to Angelica.

"Where did you get that haircut, girl? Think it would look good on this old gal here?" Angelica remembered him grinning as he referred to the body he was preparing. She looked at the woman on the dressing table. The woman had not had a haircut in years. She tried to imagine her with hair stylishly coiffured, one side longer than the other, short in the back, her neck cleanly shaved with a razor.

"Pop, she's seventy! I don't think so." Angelica had laughed, fondly kissing him on the cheek. She had run her fingers through her own hair and Pop-pop laughed with her.

At eighty-plus miles per hour, the flat Texas landscape zoomed by in a blur, dotted with the occasional roadkill. Even at that speed, there was no missing the cop standing in the center median, waving her to the side. Without checking the speedometer, she knew there was no denying how much over the speed limit she was.

Angelica slowed her car and pulled over to wait for the cop to catch up to her. She rolled down her window and waited, searching for tissues in her car to wipe back the tears that had flowed down her face for most of the two hours she had been driving.

"You okay, ma'am?"

The tears continued to roll down Angelica's face, even into her mouth. It was just her luck to be pulled over by a rocket scientist. Didn't the makeup streaming down her face make it obvious she wasn't okay?

"Everything is fine, Officer. Just peachy." Her words popped because of the salty moisture running across her lips.

The cop shifted his weight from one foot to the other, wetting his lips. One hand was on his gun holster.

"I have you at eighty-eight miles an hour in a sixty-five-mile-an-hour zone, ma'am."

She sniffed. The cop paused, obviously waiting for her to answer. Unmoved by her tears, he took out his ticket book.

"Can I have your license, registration, and proof of insurance, please?"

Angelica handed the information out the window to the waiting policeman and watched him in her sideview mirror as he walked back to his car. She couldn't speak. She knew she would sob uncontrollably if she opened her mouth again. Her Pop-pop would have been mad with her for speeding. He always reminded her to be safe, to do the responsible thing. More tears sprang to her eyes. Everything made her think of him. He was always there for her, wasn't he?

He'd taught her to drive not too long ago. Smiling through her tears, Angelica pictured him trying to give her instructions on the rules of the road, talking about female drivers the whole time as if she were exempt from the remarks he made. He was quite the joker. Now there would be no more sexist or off-color jokes from her Pop-pop. Ben Chappee III was gone.

The cop returned, handing Angelica the ticket for her signature.

"Slow down, ma'am. You sure you gonna be all right?" Another rocket-scientist-type question. There was a hole left in her heart by her grandfather's death. She wouldn't be all right for a long time. Her grandfather had raised her. He was quite strict. No dates, no nonsense, church twice a week, but they always had fun together. It was like he was protecting her from something, but he had a hell of a sense of humor. She vividly remembered the time he had tied her uncle's feet together with stockings while he was sleeping, drunk from too much vodka. He took him to the embalming room at the funeral parlor and then woke him up. Her uncle was still drunk and he thought he was paralyzed when he couldn't move his legs. Then he thought he was dead and maybe watching himself in the funeral parlor. The whole neighborhood heard him scream for Jesus! They'd laughed for weeks about that one.

The cop looked at Angelica with a peculiar expression on his otherwise nondescript face, his mouth tilted to one side as if he were preparing to spit at any moment.

"How far you going?"

"Baton Rouge." She didn't want him to think she was drunk. She wasn't even twenty-one, not yet, not for a week or so.

"Well, that's another two hours from here. Calm down and be careful. You have a nice day. Okay, ma'am?"

Angelica wiped her eyes with her disintegrated tissue and nodded. She doubted that it would be possible to have a nice day. In less than two years, she'd lost the two people who cared about her most. What was she going to do now?

Angelica thought about what her grandfather would want her to say.

"Thanks, Officer. You have a blessed day." *Blessed* was better than *nice*. Angelica rolled up her car window and pulled back onto the highway.

2

Juan lit a candle for strength. The smell from the burning wax stung his nostrils, bringing tears to his eyes. His pops was deluded. He wanted Juan to go down to Baton Rouge to handle a dry-cleaning contract. He didn't care that Juan didn't want to go. He didn't care that Juan didn't want to be involved in the family business. All his father cared about was tradition, and a *good* Hispanic boy did what he was told, even if he was twenty-five years old.

Juan didn't want to work in the stores here in the Bronx, much less go out of town to do it. He told his father that, in more ways than one.

On one hand, Juan was glad that his father had faith in him—enough faith, it seemed, to let him handle the largest contract the Delgado Brothers had ever gotten. But he hated his father for sending him to some godforsaken place he'd only heard about on TV. Didn't he know that Baton Rouge was in the South? Juan considered himself a Mandingo warrior, a master, a black Puerto Rican prince, a true Bronx-ite. Outside of the island of Puerto Rico, the Northeast U.S. was in his bones. Thank goodness the contract would only last a few weeks. Then he would be able to come back home, to the sights, sounds and colors he loved. To the unique New York flavor.

The wax from the candle began to drip down its side as Juan meditated in front of it. His father seemed to be able to read his mind from the next room. He yelled to him, disturbing the silence surrounding Juan and his thoughts.

"Make sure you have them close the books every night."

Juan didn't answer. His father clung to the old ways in the same manner he clung to his just-arrived-in-the-country accent. But Juan could not think of talking back to him. He would do as he was told. He could not think of disappointing his father and his family. It was his responsibility and his burden.

He lived at home with his family and was expected to continue living there until he got married. Even when his family had still lived in Puerto Rico, children who moved out didn't move far. Juan had a cousin who'd lived two doors down from his mother, even though he had a family of his own. Things had not changed much in the Bronx, either: His uncle lived one floor below them and used their apartment all the time as if he lived there as well. It was enough to make Juan crazy; he never brought any women home because privacy was just too hard to come by.

It seemed too easy for the Delgado Brothers to secure the

contract. Louisiana was so far away. They would be responsible for dry-cleaning the robes at the nation's largest gospel convention. People would come to Baton Rouge from all over the country. Although he'd tried to convince his father to send someone else, Juan was going to be the one to make sure things were done properly.

The Delgado Brothers had a small dry-cleaning plant down in Baton Rouge, and it was going to have to handle all of this business. They'd acquired it when his father, on the advice of a friend, bought out another small, family-owned dry cleaner through a business broker. The shop in Baton Rouge was small and it did okay. They didn't even bother to change the name or the sign outside. It still said SPOTLESS CLEANERS, the only dry cleaner in the small neighborhood. The only thing the Delgado Brothers added was a small tag on the sign that read BY DELGADO. It was so small you could almost miss it.

His family's livelihood depended on this contract and on him. Juan knew that this would make or break the family business. The saving grace of it all was that his best friend would get to go, too. James would keep him sane, if he didn't drive him crazy first.

"You lighting them damn candles again, bro?" Juan had been concentrating on his prayer and trip so hard that he didn't hear his friend barge into the room.

"Don't start, man. You know I have to ask for blessings before we go." Juan didn't turn around.

"Can you make it fast, then? We're going to miss our flight." James looked at his watch.

"We're protected, don't worry." The calmness in his voice camouflaged the dread he felt.

"Yeah, your dumb ass is protected by me." James grinned. "You better hurry it up, man. Are you packed? You got the tickets and everything?" He shifted the bag he was carrying from one hand to the other.

Juan rolled his eyes. "Yes, I do. And if you know like I know you won't hound me. You wouldn't be going without me." James was like a brother, but right now he was annoying. Sometimes he didn't know how to stop when he was ahead.

"And I wouldn't have a job, and I wouldn't have an ulcer. Just light your damn candle. Why can't you just pray normal like everyone else? You are going to be a surefire hit in the Bible Belt."

"Normal like who? You? When's the last time your behind prayed for anything other than the Super Bowl? Just chill. I'll be there in a minute." Juan turned back to his small altar and began to extinguish his candles.

"I have known you all my life, Juan, and I still can't get this religion stuff. It ain't like you go to church."

"And I am the most spiritual person you know. Hold up, let me light a candle for you, too." Juan smiled, exposing the gap between his front teeth.

"You ain't gonna be doing that in Baton Rouge, are you? You gonna chase all them southern honeys away, too. Just like the ones from here." James put his bag down and shoved it toward the door with his foot.

"Those women weren't about nothing. It won't matter to

my true spiritual partner. You'll see. I'm done anyway. What time is our flight?"

"Just get in the car, man, before you burn the place down. I'll be waiting outside." James turned and unlocked the four locks on the steel door, letting it slam behind him.

Steam rose off the hood of the van as Juan approached it. James was already in the van, waiting for it to warm up. It was March, but it was still chilly. A frost blanketed the Bronx neighborhood overnight, leaving a thin white film of ice on the windshields of all the vehicles parked on the street. The van was no exception.

The door was still locked. James reached over and opened it for Juan. The chill in the air put extra speed in his step and he was dancing as if trying to get into the car before the cold realized he was there.

Juan exhaled heavily as he plopped into the seat and slammed the van door. He rubbed his hands and watched the steam his breath made rise toward the top of the van. Juan and James made eye contact, but they did not speak immediately. James didn't attempt to drive away as Juan expected him to.

"Well?" Juan asked, raising his eyebrows. "You rushed me. So let's go."

James put both hands on the steering wheel and stared out the front window. Lately Juan snapped at him every time he spoke. He had been around the Delgado family long enough to sense when a storm was about to ensue. "Your father is coming."

Juan sucked his teeth as only he could, causing James to cringe at the sound. He was amazed every time he heard his friend do that. They'd joked about it when they were kids. The only two people alive who could make that sound into a major event were Juan and his father.

"He doesn't want us to leave the van at the airport." James sounded as apologetic as he possibly could. He knew his friend was having a disagreement with his father; he just didn't want to be in the middle of it. He'd learned from experience that the middle could be a bad place.

"We could have taken a cab." Juan crossed his arms across his chest, as if forming a shield. James would never understand. To James, this trip to Baton Rouge was an adventure. He didn't see it for what it really was: Juan's father was testing him, to see if he was capable. Juan heard his pops tell his mother that he wanted to retire, go back to Puerto Rico, of all places. The only way he could do that was if someone else could run the business. That someone else was Juan.

This wasn't news. It was expected to happen for as long as Juan could remember. The family didn't even talk about other possibilities for his future. Juan was the only son, and he was supposed to do what his father wanted. Period. The one time Juan mentioned the chance that he would do something other than run the family business, his father hit the roof. His mother cried, clutching her chest and wailing so loudly, the neighbors down the hall thought someone had died. The same thing happened every time he even mentioned moving out.

They never talked about it again. But every time he left

the house to practice his saxophone or play a gig, he could see the disappointment in his father's eyes. Big Delgado didn't have to say a word; all he had to do was look. That was enough to make Juan averse to disappointing his father or his family. They were counting on him. But that wasn't enough to keep resentment from setting in. All of his friends were free to make their own life choices. Freedom of choice was the American way everywhere else but in the Delgado household, and Juan was having a hard time being bound by a tradition started so far away.

Big Delgado opened the back door of the van and climbed in.

"When you get back, Juan, you have to repaint the name on the side of this van. The paint is chipping. And James, you better hurry up before you guys miss your flight."

Big Delgado rubbed his ungloved hands together, attempting to ward off the coldness that permeated his arthritic fingers on the short walk from the apartment building to the van. The scratching noise they emitted caused Juan to cringe. Juan sucked his teeth again and rolled his eyes. He turned on the radio. Spanish news blared out at him. He sucked his teeth again, quieter this time. Big Delgado listened only to talk radio in Spanish or WLIB, the talk radio station of Caribbean New York. It was his way of keeping in touch with what was going on in what he considered to be *his* world. Juan preferred good old R&B, and he reached forward to change the channel. He could sense his father scowl behind him as he did.

"What are you doing?" Big Delgado asked.

Juan didn't answer. Instead he turned up the volume, almost as if he were attempting to drown out the rising tension in the car. He didn't want to speak, and instead he counted to ten to help quell the anger that was seething inside him.

James put the van in gear and maneuvered out of the tight parallel parking space. He moved into traffic, and although he thought the radio was too loud, he didn't dare say a word. This was going to be one long ride to the airport.

3

The first fistful of dirt dropped from Angelica's hand into the hole in the ground. The other mourners followed suit, and she avoided eye contact with them as she turned and walked away. The way they looked at her and nodded with big open eyes made her ill. Her Pop-pop wouldn't have wanted all this sadness anyway. He'd always told Angelica that when he died he wanted a big old party, with no funeral or wake. He wanted folks to dance and laugh and celebrate all the fun he'd had while he was alive. Everyone seemed to have forgotten how often Pop-pop used to say just that. The only thing they did correctly was bury him where he wanted to be buried: by Grandma's side.

Angelica smoothed her daffodil-colored dress and looked down at the ground as she made her way back to the parking lot. All eyes were on her; the dress was form-fitting, ensuring that she stood out in the sea of people dressed in dull, lifeless black clothing. Angelica didn't care. Pop-pop wouldn't have wanted her dressed in old-lady black anyway; these folks didn't know that black was the wrong color. Pop-pop was full of so much energy that Angelica believed he was alive somewhere else for sure. They shouldn't be mourning; they should all be boogying in purple, just like he wanted.

Angelica knew in her heart that her Pop-pop's job on earth wasn't done. He had much more to learn and to teach in the universe. His spirit had to be going somewhere, maybe even coming back here.

Pop-pop used to say that Angelica was his little flower, so she wanted to look like one for him today. Besides, there was no sense in mourning him in black. All of the life in him could not have disappeared and just returned to dust. It must have changed form. Didn't her physics professor say it would? Hadn't those high school energy and science experiments proved that to her over and over again?

Most of the mourners walked away silently, moving aside for Angelica to pass as if they were afraid something they didn't want could transfer to them if they touched her in any way. That was fine with Angelica. Not wanting to talk to anyone, she'd even arrived at the funeral at the very last minute, driving herself. She'd sent the limo driver away to avoid the looks of pity from other people attending the funeral. Deep in private thought, she reminisced about her times with her grandfather. She found herself looking down at two pair of shoes, one male and one female. She tried to alter her path and step around them, but the man put his hand out and stopped her.

"Angelica," he said, "if there's anything we can do . . ."

People said the strangest things at times like these. And Angelica never understood this phrase. What could anyone possibly do to make this better? It wasn't like time could be turned back and Pop-pop could be here again. She looked up and managed to smile, realizing that she was now standing face-to-face with Pastor Davis and his wife. They were the pastoral couple at Mt. Moriah Church of the Lost Pilgrim, the church Angelica had attended all her life with her grandparents. The Davises' daughter, Ché, stood quietly behind them.

"Thank you. I'll manage. I'll be fine." At first Angelica was surprised they had come. Pastor Davis and her grandfather had not been on the best of terms since their falling out before the pastor married his new wife. A junior minister had presided over the funeral.

The pastor's wife took her hand. Angelica shrank back. Her grandmother had not been fond of the pastor's new wife. She hadn't liked her ever since she and her husband had begun choosing "Handmaidens" for the church a few years ago. They'd treated the choice as if it were some big honor, but the handmaidens were only glorified servants for the pastor's wife. Pop-pop used to say the pastor and his wife had created their own bunch of unpaid nannies and housecleaners. Folks made such a big stink about it, the Handmaidens idea finally disappeared.

"Do you know what's going to happen to the business? The funeral homes?" Pastor Davis asked. His deep voice cracked a little.

Angelica looked into the pastor's eyes and smiled. She'd been waiting for this question. She knew people were waiting to see what she was going to do, especially since she was not yet twenty-one. They were all also very concerned about Grandpa's little bit of money.

"How are things at Mt. Moriah, Pastor?"

"It must be hard for a young girl like you to think about running three funeral homes; such a large busi—"

"Three?" Where had that number come from? Sure, she knew that Pop-pop had run the only funeral home in their little side of Baton Rouge, but what had she missed? Angelica had been so busy attending music school for the past few years in the next parish that she had not paid much attention to what her grandfather was doing.

Angelica looked over Pastor Davis's shoulder and saw another gentleman approaching, one she didn't recognize. He had not been at the funeral or burial, and he was walking toward them. His stride was deliberate, heavy. He was not an ordinary mourner.

"Angelica?" he asked. He almost pushed the pastor and his wife out of the way. "I'm James Lieberman, your grandfather's lawyer. I want you to know that there will be a reading of the will tomorrow at two P.M. Your grandfather was very thorough with his instructions. Here's my card." Angelica's brows furrowed. Lieberman seemed not to breathe, speaking as if he didn't intend to use punctuation or wait for any of the small group to answer him. "I will expect you at my office."

"I am Pastor Davis." The pastor reached out his hand.

Mr. Lieberman didn't take it. "It was Mr. Chappee's wish that only Angelica be present at the reading of the will. Nice to formally meet you, Mr. Davis." Lieberman did not smile or show expression. He nodded his bald head slightly in acknowledgment.

"But surely he didn't mean me," the pastor protested. "He was part of our church family."

"Really? His instructions were very clear. I'm sorry. Angelica, I will see you tomorrow." It was a demand rather than a question.

She nodded and they watched Lieberman stride away as resolutely as he had arrived.

"Pastor, Mrs. Davis, thank you so much for your well-wishes. I am sure this will all work out." Angelica's voice sounded strained, and she tried her best to smile.

"Call me Deborah, chile." The pastor's wife offered a faultless smile, showing just enough teeth that Angelica could see that each was as perfect as the next. "After all, I'm not that much older than you. Just let us know if there is anything we can do for you, okay?" She reached out her hand and placed it on Angelica's shoulder.

Angelica looked down at it and rolled her eyes, wondering how Deborah defined "not much older." She was at least ten years older, maybe more. They seemed to have forgotten that her grandfather was not as fond of them as he once had been. Deborah drew back her hand, noting Angelica's discomfort. She ignored the look Angelica gave her. "Did you know your grandfather had such a rude lawyer?"

Angelica didn't answer immediately. Instead they all turned to watch Leiberman's car leaving the cemetery.

"Apparently there is a lot I didn't know. I'm sure I'll make sense of it all in due time." She curled her lips, attempting to smile.

"Yes, sugar, I'm sure you will." Deborah's voice was dripping with honey. The pastor now stood behind his wife, holding his daughter's hand. They both were beginning to fidget.

"I have to go. Thank you again." Angelica stepped around them and started to walk toward the parking lot to her car.

"Well, you take care. We will pray for you at Lost Pilgrim." Deborah raised her voice, as if she needed to make sure she had the last word.

As soon as Angelica was out of earshot, Deborah stopped smiling and turned to her husband. "What is wrong with that girl, Bill? She seems as strange as her grandfather was." She placed a hand on her hip.

"Why must you assume that something is wrong with her? Imagine what she is going through. She has almost no family left. Her grandmother and uncle died in the same year, and now her grandfather, too."

"But she damn sure has money," Ché said, jumping into the conversation.

"Oh, it's about time you woke up, girl. I thought you were supposed to try and be friendly with her. What happened to that?"

"Mom, I can't just jump up and be buddy-buddy with

someone to whom I have never given the time of day. It doesn't work like that. She's a few years older than I am, too. I don't see what the big deal is anyway."

They watched as Angelica's car started out of the parking lot. They were the last people in the cemetery. Their conversation paused for a moment.

"The big deal is this," Deborah said. "If she likes you, likes us, then she may be more inclined to continue what her grandfather started. To give money to the church. It's hard to say no when you know folks on a more personal level. You need to just listen to me for a change. She can be like a mentor or something. Teach you how to be rich."

"Okay, ladies. Hopefully God will just put it in her heart to take care of her church home." The pastor smoothed his suit jacket as he spoke.

"What? Have you lost your good sense, Bill?" Deborah's head moved back and forth on her shoulders. "Sometimes God needs a little help, and I plan to give it to Him. You see that girl ain't right, wearing a yellow dress to her own grandfather's funeral. Whoever heard of such a thing? She wouldn't even ride in the limousine like she was supposed to. She sent the man away, just like that. I should have used that limo if she wasn't going to." Deborah dropped a hand to her hip and gestured frantically in the air with the other. "Let's go."

"I'm sure she had her reasons, Deb. Besides, you didn't know her grandfather like I did. He was a little unconventional. He wouldn't have wanted Angelica dressed up all in black and crying and carrying on."

"Whatever. And you don't know what I know." She pointed at her husband for emphasis. "Men act like they know so much. Just get in the car and drive. Ché, I want to talk with you when we get home. We need a plan. Obviously we are going to have to help ourselves. Ain't that what you say, honey? God helps those who help themselves?"

Deborah opened her own car door and hopped into the passenger side of their SUV. She flipped down her visor, applying lipstick while looking in the mirror. "Hello-o-o? Is anybody with me? Can I get an 'Amen'?"

Neither Ché nor her father answered. Instead they looked at each other, and Ché shrugged her shoulders. Bill exhaled heavily and started the car. He got the feeling his mysterious wife would be stirring up trouble again.

4

Juan and James waited outside the office door. He swept his eyes down, across the debris-littered floor. Most places would have cleaned up if they were expecting the boss's son. Obviously not this place.

They had sifted through old plastic bags and twisted hangers to get this far. The alley outside was a mess, too. It reminded him of how much he hated this business, the business of his father and his father's father. He was constantly reminded of that. His heart was elsewhere, certainly not here in this boring, uncreative business. His talents were being wasted. His pops was not interested in hearing that, though. He never had been. Although Juan hated to admit it, he needed his father to listen. He wanted his father's blessing, even if he chose not to work in the family business.

James waited patiently for as long as he could. "So, you going in or what?"

"James, man, haven't you ever heard that silence is golden?"

"We ain't going to get the job done standing out here. Open the door, man." James motioned toward the office door.

"I'm getting my thoughts together." He dropped his voice. "You know they ain't going to be too keen on seeing me. You think they know we're Black?"

"Man, I'm Black. You? I don't know what you are. I think they know you ain't White, with a name like Juan Ali Delgado." James contorted his face and drew out Juan's surname. He surveyed the frown on Juan's face. "We all know you didn't want to come. Just be glad my cousin hooked that audition up for you while you were down here. Now you can say you played that damned saxophone all over the country."

Juan grinned. He couldn't help it: Every time he thought about playing his sax, it made him happy. Happier than almost anything else. He knew in his heart that music was where he would end up. Ever since he was a little kid, he'd loved all kinds of music. He even taught himself to read music from old books he'd borrowed from James.

The dry-cleaning business was not his calling. It was just a means to an end for him. But he just didn't have the guts to leave his family out there high and dry. Still, he didn't have a plan, at least not yet. Juan wanted to find a way to manage the family business but still follow his heart.

James looked at Juan and shook his head. He knew what it meant not to be doing what he loved. James was the one who loved the family business. Too bad he couldn't inherit it instead. James wanted it, not Juan. Juan just wanted his music, but unfortunately for him, it couldn't put food on the table or help him take care of his father in his old age. At least not yet.

James opened the door. The room inside was pretty much the same as the outside, with a little less stuff on the floor. The lighting was poor; the flickering fluorescent bulbs barely cast a dim light in the windowless room. The receptionist's desk was deserted, but Juan could hear the sounds of machines in the back. That was a good sign. At least someone was there working even if they hadn't been cleaning.

A man scurried out from the back with a quizzical look on his face. He was short and thin, with an old-fashioned handlebar mustache that was peppered with gray. He was almost completely bald and wore outdated glasses that sat on the end of his nose.

"They didn't tell me they were sending two. Which one of you is *el jefe?*" His words were spiced with a hint of a southern drawl.

He looked from James to Juan and back to James again.

Juan stepped forward. "That would be me. This is James Petri, my right-hand man. Glad to be here."

Their greeter turned and walked back into the plant quickly, gesturing for them to follow. They prepared to be properly schooled on the plan for the week. When the tour began, James was the only one who really listened, obviously very concerned with the logistics of how they were going to clean and return three hundred robes every day for a week. They were short on delivery personnel, so they would have to take up the slack themselves.

Juan's mind wandered and he found himself staring around the room time and time again. He wanted to give his friend a chance to shine. He knew James wanted to prove to the Big Delgado that he could take care of things. He was already treated like a son and he wanted the elder Delgado to know he loved the business as if he were family. And that was fine by Juan. Maybe it would help relieve some of the pressure he was feeling.

"James, why don't you set up a command center here? I'll run the deliveries."

"Really, man?"

"Sure. You know I'm a better driver. All the accidents you get into, we'd surely miss the schedule. Delivery trucks don't grow on trees."

"Man, it was just one incident." James grimaced.

"It's no sweat, James. You're better with all the logistics stuff anyway."

Juan watched the happiness spread across James's face. Driving the truck would give him time away from the office.

"You love this shit, don't ya?"

"I even love the smell of the chemicals, Jefe."

"You're crazy, man." Juan shook his head.

"Like a fox. Besides, I've been hanging around the Delgados so long, it's almost like it's in my blood."

Juan could see that James was truly in his element. He had known his friend all his life and he still couldn't understand why he loved the business so much. James saved

Juan on more than one occasion, covering for him so he could do other things.

"That ain't natural, James. If the junk they use to dry-clean were really in your blood, you'd be dead!"

"Naw, man." He winked at Juan. "If it was in my blood, I would be you."

Juan leaned back in the office chair. He crossed his legs at the ankles and placed his feet on the large brown desk. He looked around the office, which, like the rest of the plant, was in a state of disarray. Papers were piled on the desk and tacked to the peeling walls. Dust lined the computer screen. The room itself smelled like the old man who ran it, like mothballs. He put his hands behind his head and closed his eyes, imagining stages and standing ovations. He knew there was work to be done, but he didn't feel like it, and his father was not there to look over his shoulder. He felt a twinge of guilt, but was relieved not to be hounded and micromanaged by his father for a change. This week would give him a chance to sort things out.

Beyond the open door, people moved around quickly. No one spoke, but everyone seemed to be moving with a purpose. James had taken control of the room and would periodically give direction. Everyone followed his lead. Machines hissed and the room was warmed by the dry-cleaning heat to a point where almost everyone was sweating. His shirt clung to his back and was transparent, his T-shirtlessness showing through. He glanced up into the office. His eyes rested on Juan.

James's eyes narrowed. He immediately marched into the office and slammed the door behind him.

"Uh, what are you doing?" His eyes and his nostrils were wide.

Juan opened his eyes and sat forward, removing his feet from the desk. "Excuse me?"

"I said, what are you doing? There are ten thousand things to be done around here and you are sleeping." He moved forward to the front of the desk and rested on his knuckles, right in front of Juan. "What's going on, man? You sick or something?"

"Oh, no. I ain't sick. I was taking a break." Juan ran his hand through his curly hair. "Okay with you?"

"No, it's not. I know your heart ain't in it, but let's not start taking advantage."

"You got it under control, right?"

James slammed his fist down on the desk. "I got it, but that don't mean I don't need you. You are an ungrateful—"

"Uh, keep your voice down, man!" Juan rolled the office chair closer to the desk. "I was about to review some of this paperwork. You know I'm also supposed to review the books."

James was losing his patience. "Review the books doesn't mean sleep. You take everything your father does for you for granted—"

Juan pushed his chair back forcefully and stood. He walked around the desk and James turned to face him. "What would you know about it? About what fathers should do, huh? You don't live my life!"

James drew back. His heart sank. "Oh, you don't have to go there. So what? My daddy left when I was two. Your father is the closest thing to one that I have, and I am not going to sit here any longer and see you take advantage of him. You need to get yourself together and make some decisions. He is hardworking and he just wants the best for you. The minute he's out of sight, you act like that ain't worth anything! If you're going to be a man, then be one, but don't sleep."

Juan paused a minute. He was used to his friend being a pain in the butt, but he was not used to him calling him on the carpet like this. "So what are you saying?" He hung his head down. James was right. He had to make some decisions soon or things would only get worse. "I'm sorry, man."

James dropped his voice. "I'm saying that you need to get it together so we can get our job done. It is *our* job, not just mine, until you and your father work it out otherwise." He put his hand on his friend's shoulder. "Don't you realize that your dad might not have many years left? That all you have to do is what he wants for a while? After that, you can sell the business or have someone else run it or whatever. Don't you realize how fortunate you are?"

Juan sat back on the desk and dropped his head. James had always supported him over the years, through thick and thin. He knew in his heart that James would not steer him wrong.

"Look, I know both of you. Do a good job here, it will be easier for your folks to listen to you. Doesn't he always say that you can catch more flies with honey than with vinegar?"

"I'm sorry, James. My bad. Let's get it together. I didn't mean to upset you. You're right, we don't have a whole lot of time." He stood up and walked over to the door.

James followed. "I made a list of what we have to do first to coordinate all this." He reached into his pocket. "First you need to lose your bad attitude."

Juan laughed. He knew James had his back. He admired the way James saw light in every situation. It was only a week, but when the week was up, he was going to really talk to his father for a change.

5

Angelica looked down at the business card in her hand. She was at the right address. She hadn't known there were any offices down here. She thought it was all factories. This building was almost hidden behind the old Spotless Cleaners plant.

Angelica hesitated in front of the worn door, smelling the chemicals from the plant. She glanced over at Jeanette, her best friend since she was six years old. She looked as worried as Angelica did, but Angelica was glad she'd asked to come, against the lawyer's wishes. The support felt good. It probably wasn't necessary; Angelica knew Pop-pop would not have left any loose ends. He'd always taken care of business so well while he was alive, there was probably nothing to fear.

She was still surprised to find out that there was more than one funeral home. She'd thought the one in their neighborhood was all her Pop-pop had owned. Pop-pop never mentioned any others to her at all. He occasionally traveled, but he never took Angelica with him. It was almost as if he didn't want her to worry about adult things. She smiled, remembering the way he would rub her head and tell her that the only thing she had to worry about was school. He wouldn't even let her have a part-time job in the office. She now knew that Pop-pop had run three funeral homes in Louisiana. Angelica had been so busy with her head in her music sheets that she was totally ignorant of the things that were right under her nose all along.

The pastor and his wife seemed to have been a little insulted by Mr. Lieberman. It was no wonder; they probably thought they deserved a little piece of the funeral home pie, even expected it. Angelica knew Pop-pop was a big giver to his church. The things that went on there often annoyed him, but he believed and participated in the church. That church was his politics, and he and the pastor used to be good friends. They still called him out every week as a regular tither, too. For that reason, Angelica knew they were sad to see him go. He was supporting the church. The funeral home business was lucrative. Pop-pop used to say he was guaranteed business; everybody had to die. She smiled to herself as she thought about the number of times he had told her that.

Angelica walked into the brightly lit office and looked around, noting the series of signed and numbered lithographs on the wall and the plush leather furniture. It was evident from the furniture that Mr. Lieberman was not doing too bad himself. Angelica did not doubt that her grandfather was one of his biggest clients.

There was no receptionist. Angelica was not surprised. No one in Baton Rouge worked on Sunday. Mr. Lieberman came from the back of the office in long, lanky strides. It looked as if his knees were on the back of his skinny legs, reminding Angelica of a giraffe.

He took Angelica's hand between his own and looked from her to Jeanette. His mouth was drawn into a thin line, his lips almost disappearing. The clasp of pity. She knew that most of the time it was false, and she was immediately wary of this man. She surmised that his attempt at condolences seemed to be as false as most of the people she'd encountered over the past few days. He dropped her hand quickly, without offering the customary *I'm so sorry.* It was as if he felt discomfort with what he was about to do.

"You were supposed to come alone."

Angelica opened her mouth to speak, but Jeanette interrupted her. "You know it is deserted and things get crazy down here on the weekends. I just came to support my girl, that's all. I don't need to know nothing. I'll just wait out here . . . if that is okay with you?" She rolled her eyes and stood her ground.

Lieberman paused, staring at Jeanette but not speaking. His eyes were trying to avoid her too-short skirt and multicolored nails. He didn't bother to answer her; he could tell she really didn't care whether he thought it was okay or not.

"We're ready. Follow me."

Jeanette nodded and sat on the leather sofa, immediately reaching for a *People* magazine on the side table. Lieberman seemed satisfied and loped away, Angelica following him, taking three steps to each of his. She resisted the urge to mock the way he walked. She could almost see her grandfather making fun of the way he walked, Laurel-and-Hardy-style, as he led her into a conference room that was walled in glass. The longest table Angelica had ever seen was in the center of the room. Lieberman motioned for her to sit, moving over to stand beside a TV and VCR standing on a rolling cart.

"Well, thank you for coming at the appointed time. Your grandfather left a video of his will. He wanted there to be no mistakes. His wishes were that you view the video of his will exactly one day after his burial."

Angelica raised her eyebrows. Technology had certainly invaded everything. She didn't expect to be viewing a video today, but she should have known her grandfather would go for the unconventional.

Mr. Lieberman turned on the television and VCR and pressed play. He did not move from beside the television stand as the screen flickered to life. Angelica smiled as the form of her grandfather appeared on the screen in his favorite jacket. She recognized the background in the video immediately. It was obviously taped in their own living room. Her Pop-pop sure loved his gadgetry; they even had automatic blinds in their house and Pop-pop could turn lights on from the funeral home with his computer.

The video began.

"Angelica, I am sorry I had to leave you, baby. The shame

of it all is I couldn't embalm myself. Did they do me justice? You know how I like my hair combed straight back."

The tears started to flow from Angelica's eyes, but she couldn't help but laugh a little through her tears. She nodded and took a tissue from the box on the table.

"I was the best in town. No one prepared folk to meet their maker like I did, ain't that right?" Angelica dabbed at her eyes and laughed again. He was still joking, even in death.

"This is my last will and testament, girl, and it is real simple. I am of sound mind and body. Mr. Lieberman is the executor of my estate. That means it's his job to see that all my wishes get carried out. I have faith that he will.

"My wishes are straight and to the point. Angelica, you have been the light of my life and your grandmother's life for a long time. It broke our heart when your parents died, and after that you became everything to us. You were such a wonderful child, all I had left after your grandmother went on."

Angelica felt again the panic and despair as she remembered being left alone after her parents passed away. They had died when she was five years old, their car hit when a teenage drunk driver ran a stop sign at fifty miles an hour on the way home from a school dance. They were killed instantly.

"I wish to leave everything to you, all my worldly possessions. That includes the three funeral homes in Louisiana, the cars, the boat, and the house." He paused. Angelica's eyes were round as saucers.

"I know I wasn't very good about including you in the

business, but I wanted to shield you from all that, from all the greed I saw around me. You know people will do just about anything for money. We talked about it all the time, and I didn't want you to grow up to be a spoiled 'trust-fund baby.' There is one condition. You have been a good girl and I believe in my heart that I raised you right. I always taught you to be true to yourself, and now is the time for you to show us all what is truly in your heart. I know you've been saving yourself, but I think you need to experience life. All this is yours on the condition that you lose your virginity within six days, and it must be verified by the family physician." Pop-pop paused again, seemingly for a reaction from Angelica.

Angelica's head snapped up and she looked in the direction of Mr. Lieberman. He had not moved nor blinked, even when his name was mentioned.

"What? I thought he said he was of sound mind!" Angelica's heart thumped in her chest. Her pulse was racing. The video continued.

"I am just fine, Angelica. I think you have been too sheltered, and that is my own fault. You have six days, at the end of which you come back here to hear the rest of this tape." The screen went black.

Angelica sat, eyes and mouth open wide. She couldn't believe it. Pop-pop had spent years chasing away boys, and now he was giving her free rein to go out and get it on or she got no money. How could he do this? It must be another one of his jokes. Mr. Lieberman interrupted her thoughts.

"Your grandfather's wishes are very clear. We discussed it extensively."

"How much money are we talking about?"

"About two-point-three million dollars plus real estate. You should be pretty well taken care of the rest of your life. It will be set up in trusts and so forth, to ensure it is protected for you, but we can discuss that later."

Angelica tried to read Lieberman, but no emotion registered on his face. He handed her a sheet of paper.

"I'm sure you know this, but here is the name and address of the family physician. I have taken the liberty of making an appointment for you, per your grandfather's instructions. On the sixth day, he will verify that you are no longer a virgin. You are still a virgin, right?"

"Of course I am! I can't believe you even asked me that!" She rolled her eyes.

"Well, come back here, then, no matter what the outcome, and we will view part two of the tape." Lieberman shook Angelica's hand and loped out of the room.

Angelica was confused as a barrage of mixed emotions raced through her heart and mind. How could Pop-pop do something like this? He'd preached at her all her life about being a good girl, and now this? She couldn't believe it. What was she going to do? Two-point-three million dollars was a lot of money. If she played her cards right, with that kind of money she could live fairly decent for a long time. She could be the singer she wanted to be and not worry about eating. She couldn't just let that go.

She couldn't deny that there were times she had come

close to losing her virginity. There were a few secret dates, and there were definitely a few times when desire almost got the best of her. Most of the men involved would never speak to her again after she let them get all hot and bothered and then changed her mind. She would be too embarrassed to call them now . . . but then again, how hard could it be?

Angelica began recovering from her shock and smiled to herself as she left the office. She couldn't decide whether to be happy or sad. She was beginning to think that it was time anyway. Her birthday was coming up soon; she would be twenty-one years old. Maybe this wasn't such a bad deal.

When Angelica returned to the waiting room, Jeanette stood, tugging at her skirt in an attempt to bring it back down to more acceptable levels. Angelica shook her head; no amount of pulling was going to help that skirt. Angelica was sure that if Jeanette bent over, it would be possible to see her panties and the beginnings of her butt cheeks. Jeanette's clothing was a direct contrast to her character. The two friends were probably the only two virgins in their high school graduating class. Jeanette opened her mouth and Angelica held up her hand.

"Outside." Angelica could not talk about this now. Jeanette would have a thousand questions for her on the ride home.

Six days. Angelica needed to go home and check out the situation, review her book of phone and address numbers. She needed to come up with a plan on how and with whom she was going to get it on. She might as well enjoy coming into her own.

6

The motel was small but clean, just like the Motel 6 commercials said it would be. It wasn't fancy, but it would do for their purposes, and they each had their own rooms for the price of one at the larger hotels. The motel sat off a frontage road paralleling Interstate 10, about eight miles from the dry-cleaning plant and downtown. It was on the outskirts of Port Allen, Louisiana, not far from Alligator Bayou.

Juan had smirked when he heard the name; he was disappointed when it didn't look like the swamp he imagined it would. He'd expected people in long boats poling their way through the murky water, hats made of nutrea fur atop their heads. Instead he saw only stretches of highway with water somewhere underneath, not visible from the road. He doubted there could really be any alligators in there at all. But where the parking lot ended, weeds began, and instead of the city sounds that Juan was used to waking up to, he awoke to the din of insects and a green, wet smell that was unfamiliar, but good.

James and Juan did not share a room in case one of them had to "entertain," as James put it. Juan's room was on the second floor almost directly above James's. As he got out of the shower and checked his appearance in the mirror, Juan wondered if his friend had slept well. Sleep had put Juan in a better frame of mind and he wanted to get to the plant bright and early. He turned his face from side to side and smiled at his reflection as he smoothed his well-shaped goatee. His cocoa-brown skin was flawless and the features of his otherwise clean-cut face blended well together and told of his African and Spanish ancestry. His hair arranged itself into curls as he ran his hand through it. He tried to make his one piece of straight hair lay down, knowing it never would. His hair had a mind of its own, and unlike his father, Juan had come to accept that not everyone or every-thing could see things his way.

Juan felt better today about his purpose than he had when he'd first arrived in Baton Rouge. He smoothed his perfectly creased uniform shirt. Today he would have to wear the uniform of a delivery driver, but that was okay. He was going to be the smoothest dry-cleaning delivery man Baton Rouge had ever seen.

He'd grown up in the dry-cleaning business, and he wore many hats over the years, from cashier to accountant. His father believed that hands-on was the best way to learn the business. What Juan had learned best was that he hated al-most all the jobs. But it would be okay; light was at the end of the tunnel. He felt almost ready to break away and explore his music. He was ready to take a chance. Almost.

Juan pocketed the room's key card and walked down the outside flight of stairs to James's door. He knocked and inhaled the morning smells. He smiled. The South smelled good; he had to admit to himself that he almost liked this part of it. He knocked again, and then shrugged when James's door did not fly open. It was just like him to get a head start on things. He probably had not slept at all, but instead spent the night making plans for the week.

Juan found his way to the plant alone without incident. He sifted his way through the debris in the alleyway outside the plant, expecting to be among the first there. Things were already humming. James sat at the reception desk, which was now covered with papers. The smell of fresh coffee mixed in with the familiar dry-cleaning chemical odor. James appeared to be well-engrossed in the day's business already.

"Hey, man. What's up? You didn't waste any time, did you? Did you even sleep?"

"You know what they say, Jefe. The early bird gets the worm. Coffee for you." He handed Juan a large paper cup from Starbucks.

"I hope it ain't that weak-ass American blend shit that you drink, amigo. You know I only like the real deal."

"Dude, you know me better than that. The details are what's important. Nothing but Jamaican Blue for you. Plus those sissy scone things you like, too."

"Call them what you like, but you just haven't been able

to appreciate the finer things in life, James." He sipped the coffee from the hot cup and grimaced. It was still very hot.

"Yeah, yeah. I know I ain't like you. Seems to me that you overlook the forest for all those finer things. I appreciate what's important, though. Look here. I've already lined up today's pickups and deliveries for you. This thing is spread out among several hotels. You'll be handling three. Think you can deal, man?" James spread a worksheet on the desk.

"You know I keep a level head. Bring it on."

"Oh, yeah, that is one of your commandments, right?" James grinned.

"Don't go there, man. You know yourself that power resides in a cool head." Juan sipped his coffee, grimacing at the taste. Although it was his favorite, the taste always shocked him.

"Well, you must be one powerful brother, 'cause nothing ever seems to get you upset. You were even cool when you got dumped last month." He snickered. "Man, she was fine. How did you mess that one up?"

"Why you have to go there? You don't even know what happened." Juan sucked his teeth.

James smiled. "Something wrong with the coffee, man? We got raw sugar over there, since I know you don't like anything refined." He motioned toward a small folding table in the corner. "And you ain't tried to clue me in yet, have you? What *is* the deal? What would make you let a fine sister like Sabrina leave?"

"The coffee is just right. And it ain't your business. What makes you think I was the one who did something anyway? Besides, I am not ready to talk about it, okay? Just give me my delivery list."

James handed the three-page list to Juan.

"Do you think you could have given some of these instructions to me verbally?" He rifled through the pages. "You wrote down every detail. You're as bad as Papi. Did you tell me when to go to the bathroom, too?"

"You know we need to get this right. I was just trying to make it as easy as possible for you. Just make sure you get the right robes to the right people, okay?"

"I got it under control." Sometimes James overplanned, he thought. Juan stuffed the list into his pants pocket. "Just let me finish this coffee. I may need it—it's going to be one long day."

"And night. We're going to need your cool head, and a lot of others just like it, to get through this, man."

James watched as Juan left the plant. This was not only going to be a long day, it was going to be a long week. He knew he would have to work long and hard to keep Juan motivated, but it was for the guy's own good.

Big Delgado did not pay much, but James enjoyed the work, even though his mother complained about it often. She wanted him to go out and get a civil service job, something that would guarantee him a little security. He glanced at his watch. He had not called home yet, although he promised he would. He sighed and picked up the phone, dialing all the numbers of his mother's phone number and calling card without a pause.

The phone rang six times before his mother finally answered it. She didn't bother to say hello. "Why you wait so long to call me?" Her words slurred together.

"You drinking already, Ma?" James couldn't believe his ears. "It isn't even ten in the morning!"

"Don't you worry about what I do. I am the mother. I guess you arrived safely, huh? I can't believe you went all the way down South for them folk. They don't pay you nothing."

"They pay me enough, Ma. You don't worry about me, okay?" James flipped through the papers on his desk. "Besides, Juan is my friend."

"A friend would pay you more."

James ignored the sound of ice clinking in her glass. He didn't want to start an argument with his mother. "He doesn't have any control over it. I get paid the same as anyone else who does the same job I do. Do I have any mail?"

"Hmpph. Does Juan get paid what you do? I bet not. I can't keep carrying you forever, you know. Yeah, you got mail. Something here from the post office. You gonna take the job if they are offering you one? They got good benefits."

James paused for a minute to measure his words. He could tell that his mother was well on her way to being drunk again. He let her comment slide. He was carrying her, but he was supposed to, she was his mother. He couldn't afford two apartments at New York prices, so she lived with him. He didn't want to argue, just make sure that she was all right. "Ma, why are you pressuring me about taking some dead-end job? I told you how I feel about that. I just applied to make *you* happy. I don't think I would be happy at a place where I was not rewarded for being the best. I don't want to work somewhere where I just gotta hang on to get a pension. What kind of a life is that?" He took a quiet breath and began to count to ten silently.

"I just want the best for you, baby boy. And those jobs ain't dead-end. I told you. I worked for the post office myself for—"

"I know, Ma, for fifteen years. And look where it got you. You got nothing to show but carpal tunnel and a habit." James looked up as the dispatch radio stirred to life. "I gotta go, someone's calling me. I'll see you soon." He didn't wait for his mother to reply. He hung up the phone and shook his head. He was going to have to work like crazy this week, but would enjoy his time away.

7

Deborah sifted through her closet for just the right dress to wear to the conference. Nothing seemed to be just right. She yelled to her daughter.

"Ché! Have you been in my closet again? I can't find some of my suits." Deborah was late and annoyed. Ché had a habit of wearing her clothes without asking. And she never returned them. The lack of any answer intensified Deborah's frustration. She continued to talk, seemingly to an empty house.

"You know I gotta look right for this conference, girl. Our church has the biggest choir. We are going to win this thing, and how will it look if my clothes look all messed up? I *am* the pastor's wife."

Deborah found a green wool suit. She fingered it lightly. Finally, just the look she wanted. Refined but not fussy. These other folk in the church didn't know anything about finer clothes. This suit made her look good even on her

worst days. Fine clothes hide a multitude of sins. Her husband didn't understand that, or the amount of money she
spent on her clothes. It made her feel good, like she was almost making up for being raised with so little. And good
clothes fit better, too, they were more forgiving. Lately she
had been eating a lot, as she did when there was so much
on her mind.

She glanced down at her watch as she slipped on the suit.
She turned slightly in the walk-in closet, and admired herself in the full-length mirror set in one wall. Deborah always
looked so together, years younger than other women her
age. Her straight hair was perfectly cut into a chin-length
bob that accentuated her heart-shaped face. The hair seemed
to curl under just right, pointing to the "beauty mark," as
her mother called it, that was just to the right of her lips, and
highlighting her almond-shaped light brown eyes.

She became aware of Ché standing in the doorway,
watching her admiring her shape. "How long you been
standing there? You know better than to sneak up on me."
Deborah walked into her bathroom.

"You talking to yourself again, Ma? I just got here. Are
you ready to go yet? We're going to be late for the opening
session of the conference." Ché finished applying her trade-
mark eye liner on her otherwise unadorned face. She
wanted to make her eyes look as attractive as her mother's.

"How do I look?" Deborah turned slightly so that her
daughter could take in the whole picture presented before
her, not really wanting her to answer. She knew she looked
good, and she ran her hand over her behind and admired

the way the skirt draped on it. "I've been thinking. Look here, this is the plan. We need to get some money for the church." Deborah grabbed a hairbrush and waved it at Ché. "Angelica is the one to give it to us."

"You've been thinking, huh? Scheming is more like it." Ché rolled her eyes. Her mother was always up to something. "Why should she? I told you before—"

"And I told you, I do the telling around here. You need to make her trust you. Besides, I deserve it." Deborah turned and looked in her vanity mirror. She dabbed at her hair with the brush. It was already perfect.

"Everything is always about you, isn't it, Ma? What about the church? Isn't that what you mean?" Deborah always put herself first, and Ché could not remember a time when Deborah had asked her what she thought and meant it.

"Don't talk back to me. I am still your mother. And you know I meant the church. The church deserves it. You just do as I say, okay?"

Ché pursed her lips. Her mother always found a way to make Ché part of her plans, whether she wanted to be or not. "How am I supposed to make her trust me? And even if she does, why should that make her give money?" She snatched the brush from her mother and started brushing her own hair with it.

"You are just getting too big for your own britches, girl." Deborah gave her daughter a sharp look. "You will just ask her. Tell her that the church needs money. We can name a wing or something after her grandfather. That was the plan before he died anyway."

Ché put her hands on her hips. Her mother was something else and getting nuttier by the minute. If she wasn't scheming on someone, she was forever thinking someone was scheming on her.

"Have the trustees agreed to that, Ma?"

"Not yet, but they will. I can convince your stepfather to ask them for anything. He doesn't need to know the details. He will think it was his own idea when I'm done with him. And you go put on a slip, okay? Everybody does not need to see your business."

Ché was silently surprised at her mother's determination. She didn't answer, but went to her room to hunt down a slip. Her mother worried so much about what people thought, but she always looked so cool on the outside.

Ché had never given much thought to Angelica before; the girl always kept pretty much to herself. Angelica always sat with her grandfather in church, not socializing, especially these past few months. She didn't attend any of the teen or young adult events and she didn't even lip-sync in the choir. She just hung out with that friend of hers, Jeanette. They were both strange ones. It was almost as if Angelica did not want to fit in or be like anyone else. She even looked different. Angelica didn't even straighten her sandy brown hair, choosing instead to let it remain bushy and untamed. Most of the time, Angelica wore her hair tied into one long braid that fell heavily in the middle of her back.

Getting Angelica to trust her was going to be difficult. Ché searched her mind for a connection, an opportunity for them to strike up a conversation, but was unable to see one. She wished she understood her mother's motives, but she'd given up trying to understand her mother a long time ago.

Ché found a half slip and put it on under her skirt. She looked in the mirror and checked the view from the back. She really did not need a slip, but it would make her mother happy. She was being strange since Ben Chappee died and Ché did not want to set her off. Deborah was always secretive, even with Ché. Ché knew nothing about her, not really, except that they had no family to speak of. Her mother would never talk about what family she knew of, if she knew of any. Ché didn't even know much about her own natural father. Her mother only said that she loved him very much but they couldn't be together, like Romeo and Juliet. Ché used to think that was so romantic. Now she just thought it was weird. She walked back into her mother's room.

"Ready, Ma?"

Deborah was sitting on a chair by the window. She jumped as Ché entered. She closed a small book that she was reading and covered it with her hand. It was cloth-covered and appeared to be worn and fraying in several places.

"Didn't I tell you to stop sneaking up on me, girl?"

"I wasn't Ma. You told me to go get a slip!"

Ché watched as her mother placed the book back into a wooden box that she kept on her nightstand and locked it. Ché wondered what was in the book. She'd caught her mother reading it several times recently.

She turned around so her mother could check her out

from behind. "That's much better. Shouldn't have any panty lines. I thought I taught you that."

"You did, Ma." She glanced at her watch. "Can we go?"

Deborah picked up her compact, reapplying her foundation for the fifth time since she'd gotten dressed.

"You watch Oprah just the same as I do. You should never go anywhere without a good slip and those butt-smoother things I bought you."

Ché rolled her eyes, glancing at the box that contained the book. "Ain't it time to go?"

"Didn't I tell you not to say *ain't*?" Deborah gave her an assessing look, making sure the match between her shoes and her bag was exactly right.

"Yes, Ma, you did." Ché felt as if she could never do anything right in her mother's eyes.

"That's right. And you should learn to listen to your mother. Let's go. They're waiting."

Ché didn't have the energy to ask her mother who *they* were. She would probably just get a lecture about how they should look or something. Instead, she followed Deborah out of the bedroom and to the car.

8

Angelica slept hard, formulating a game plan in her dreams. By the time she awoke, she thought she had pieced together a plan to get her inheritance. The best and fastest way to lose her virginity would be to call someone up and just do it. It wasn't going to be easy; she didn't know a lot of men outside of Mt. Moriah. She didn't know a lot of men inside of Mt. Moriah, either, at least not ones who got her juices flowing or were at least halfway attractive. She rubbed her eyes, remembering how her grandfather would step between her and any male who even halfway looked her way. "He ain't worth it," he would say. "You better make sure it's right. And he ain't." It didn't matter who it was, no one ever would have been right in his eyes.

Her thoughts were interrupted by someone ringing the doorbell, followed by a muffled pounding at her door. She hopped out of bed, walked the two steps to the small love seat in her bedroom, and grabbed her robe as the doorbell chimed "The Yellow Rose of Texas." She smiled; the chime was a little over the top, but her grandfather loved it. He'd installed it himself. She wrapped the robe around her body and headed for the front door. She knew it was Jeanette; she would be the only person to come to her house without calling first.

When she opened the door, Jeanette greeted her with a tentative look on her face. She leaned up against the doorjamb with one hand on each side, as if Angelica could not get the door open fast enough. Her hair was plastered to her head, slicked down in finger waves that framed her brown face, and although it was early in the morning, her short skirt and makeup suggested that she was ready for a long night.

"You okay?" Angelica nodded and Jeanette barged past her into the front room. "Well, you better fill me in, then. I can't believe you made me wait this long. You don't look too upset anymore. I couldn't figure out what was going on yesterday. When we left that lawyer's office, you looked somewhere between pissed off and amazed. What's the deal?"

Her tennis skirt was so short that Angelica could almost see her underwear as she walked. But this was normal for Jeanette. She had a wild streak that came out only in her clothes.

Jeanette flopped down on the green sectional and crossed her legs as Angelica closed the door.

"Well," she said. "You are not going to believe this, but *I* am getting an inheritance." Angelica prepared herself for the barrage of questions she refused to answer before.

"Well, we knew that. You always were a prima donna. Did you think you weren't going to be taken care of? Ben loved his girl!" Jeanette smirked. She often used Angelica's grandfather's first name, much to Angelica's chagrin. Sometimes she'd even slipped and did it in his presence. Angelica knew there was no disrespect intended, though; Jeanette had loved Ben as if he was her own grandfather.

Angelica ignored Jeanette's lame remarks. Her friend had been such a trooper, trying extra hard to keep her mind off things the past few days.

"There's a catch." She sat on the couch with her friend. "I have to lose my virginity *this week* to get it."

Jeanette's mouth dropped open. "Excuse me?"

"You heard right."

"Are we talking about the same man? The man who wanted you to go to an all-girl's high school? The man who would barely let you date? What happened? Are you going to do it? Is this for real? What's your plan?"

"Well, I'm not sure. I even dreamed about it." Angelica stood up and walked into the kitchen.

Jeanette followed her. "Are they sure he was sane? He seemed all right to me last time I saw him."

"The lawyer assured me he was." She shrugged. "And it's a lot of money. I need it, you know I do. I was going to tell him that I wanted to go to New York, to go to Juilliard. They can't teach me anything new in that music school here. I know he wanted me to stick around and maybe take more of an interest in the funeral business, but I just ain't with that. And with the money, if I can get in, I'll be able to go to school and not worry about working or money or anything." She opened the stainless steel refrigerator and removed a carton of orange juice.

"You never had to worry about money. Worry would have done you in. You're not tough like I am. Construction is a tough business. How many times did Ben have to help my family out? I remember him always being there for us."

Jeanette's father had been a construction worker for many years, and when the building business was down, he was often out of work. Angelica's grandfather helped many times, without even being asked.

"You know you should have gone straight to college anyway," Jeanette continued. "I said y'all had too much money to begin with. Only rich people let their children take off from school to 'find themselves' like you wanted to. I can't believe you would consider doing what he's asking. What happened to 'saving yourself' and all that?" Jeanette reached into a cabinet and grabbed a glass to serve herself some orange juice.

"Saving myself for what? That seems pointless now. My parents and my grandfather were always planning for futures they didn't get to have. It's obvious there are no guarantees, and I would hate to go before I got a chance to— "

Jeanette held up her hand. "Don't even go there."

"The real deal was, I was being a chicken." She looked down at the ground and turned to face the counter. "I heard it hurts. I was just telling you all that stuff about saving myself for marriage." She grabbed a sponge and wiped at some nonexistent spill.

"C'mon. I have known you forever. The real deal is that Ben would have killed you—after he made you have a shotgun wedding. And it ain't that bad." She winked.

"Whatever." Angelica waved her hand, dismissing Jeanette's remarks. "Wait, what? I thought you never—"

"I never said I never. You didn't ask, so I didn't tell you when it happened. You were the one that was so adamant about abstaining."

It was Angelica's turn to stand there with her mouth agape. "I thought we shared everything. I can't believe you were withholding information from me! After all we have been through. You know that ain't right!" Her voice became whiny. "I would have told you!"

"No, you wouldn't have." Jeanette shook her head. "There are some things you just don't tell. And I never spoke to him again anyway." She glanced away.

The kitchen was silent for a minute, the air filled with the sound of the clock ticking. Angelica searched Jeanette's face.

"Are you going to help me or what?"

"If that's what you want. You know I'm going to be there for you." They laughed. "Well, I don't really want to be *there*, you know what I mean. You can just fill me in on all the details."

"Oh, so you want *me* to share?" Angelica raised an eyebrow.

"You have to now, you know. I *know* the deal."

The two girls hugged and headed back to Angelica's bedroom. It was still decorated the same as it was when she was five: pink ruffles on a canopied bed piled high with the stuffed animals and dolls from her childhood. The windows were covered with lightweight matching pink curtains. A small dressing table sat off to the side, filled with nail polish bottles and lined with perfume, and a black love seat sat next to the window and across from the small bed.

Angelica reached into the drawer on the dressing table and brought out a little black book. She flipped through it, realizing that it was filled with mostly the names of women she knew. There were a few men, but for most she wouldn't even shake their hand, much less sleep with them.

Jeanette interrupted her search. "What are you doing?"

"Looking for a candidate." She held the book open in her hands. Jeanette removed it from her hands, flipping through it herself.

"You know that is not going to work. You got anything other than choirboys in here? Your whole church will be in your business, and that dragon lady pastor's wife will be leading the pack."

Jeanette was right. The whole idea was strange to Angelica, and she wanted her first time to be special. Was she really willing to give that up?

But the facts were plain: she needed that money. Her own parents had not left her anything. They did not have the foresight to take care of their wills or any part of their estates before they were killed in the car crash.

Angelica was only five when it had happened. She did not

remember a thing. She knew the story, though. It was a favorite topic of discussion at Mt. Moriah. Everyone loved to talk about how wonderful her grandfather was, taking in poor, penniless Angelica after her parents died. It was a two-sided compliment. Her grandfather was especially nice, they said, because her mother was not even really his daughter, though she had been born right after Angelica's grandparents were married. How would they know? Over the years, Angelica heard enough speculation about who the church members thought her blood grandfather was. Her grandparents had been happy together over the years and didn't talk about it, so the gossipmongers in their circle filled in the story with made-up details that changed all the time.

The pastor's wife was the biggest talker. No sooner had she come to town than her jaw started wagging, jumping right in on the church gossip like she had a right. She had nerve; her daughter, Ché, was not the pastor's blood daughter, either. Supposedly, her real father was also a pastor, but he left the town they'd lived in under shady circumstances and was never heard from again. At least that was the story she let get told. It seemed too convenient.

"You just can't call someone up and say, *Hey, you want to get it on so I can get paid?* That will never work," Jeanette declared.

Angelica thought about the logistics of her task. "You're probably right. Most of them would probably want a cut or something."

"Or try to stick around for a while. You don't want to get hooked up with a Klingon."

Angelica knew Jeanette was talking not so much about *Star Trek*, but about guys who stayed beyond their welcome. That would not be a good thing. She was going to have to do this without anyone knowing her motivation.

Six days was not a long time. Angelica took her book back and looked at it closer. If she was successful, she could have one hell of a birthday party. If not, she would have to start looking for a job, and the thought of going to Juilliard or any other music school would be out the window.

A possibility suddenly leaped out at her from the book she held.

"How about him? What do you think?"

Jeanette stopped fiddling with Angelica's bottles of nail polish and looked over Angelica's shoulder. "Who? David? Really? You can't be serious?"

"David Mitchell used to go to Sunday School with me when we were kids. When we were twelve, he kept getting in trouble for pulling my hair and teasing me more than once. Didn't that mean he liked me?"

"Maybe so, but that was years ago. And he has an eye in the middle of his forehead!" David seemed to have one zit perpetually centered on his forehead.

"You're stupid. I don't have to look at him too long anyway. I'm going to call him."

Jeanette stuck out her tongue, making a face as Angelica sat on the bed. Angelica's hands trembled as she dialed the phone. How hard could it be? People did it all the time, and on the first date, too. How hard could it be for a sister to get some love?

Get Some Love

The phone rang and she held her breath, counting off the rings the way the Count used to on Sesame Street. She remembered David tugging her hair. He stopped coming to Sunday School the next year, preferring instead to hang out with his friends. He was kind of cute then, but had developed a horrible case of acne, so bad his face was left looking like Swiss cheese.

Just as she was about to hang up, he answered the phone. "Hello?"

"Hi, Dave. It's Angelica. From church."

Jeanette slapped her hand over her mouth in the background.

"It's David, not Dave. Yeah?"

"How are you?" *Whatever.* He was already annoying her. Dave or David, what was the difference? The lights would be off and she could close her eyes. "I was wondering if you would be interested in going out."

"Excuse me? Going out where? Are you okay? I don't understand."

"You know, out. Date. Movies, dinner, my treat."

The phone was silent. Angelica could hear the clock ticking in the background, her six days counting away. Jeanette stood behind her, hand still over her mouth, holding her breath. Angelica fidgeted in her seat and looked at her wristwatch. She tapped her fingers on the table. "Well?"

"Sure, sure. Where? Do you want me to pick you up?" Angelica could hear a light bulb turn on as David's voice softened and became more intimate. He was already trying to be a "Mack-daddy." *Pul-eeze!*

She had not thought past the actual asking-out part of the date. What were they going to do? Where were they going to do the deed? If he picked her up, that would give her time to think of the rest. She would have to play it by ear.

David interrupted the awkward pause on the phone. "Did I mention that I've been called to go to the seminary? My meaning on earth has been shown to me. We can talk about it on our date."

Angelica blinked, feeling silly. This was a bad idea, a wrong choice. She didn't remember that about him. She didn't even remember seeing him in church, other than Sunday School. Besides, if he were really going to be a minister, David would be shopping for a wife. There weren't very many single ministers, and not one in her church. She would never get rid of him if she even tried to breathe the same air. Angelica could feel it in her bones. If she offered to sleep with him in the short time she had, he would be declaring her destined for hellfire and brimstone for sure. He might not even want to sleep with her now that he was going into the ministry. She could be wasting her time.

"Oh, Dave, it just occurred to me, isn't there a church event tomorrow? I almost forgot. Don't you have to be there?" Angelica abruptly hung up the phone. *What was she thinking?*

Jeanette threw her hands up in the air in disbelief. "What happened? You were doing good."

"I need to rethink this. He said he's going to be a minister now. That's not good."

She stood up, pacing back and forth in her small room as

Jeanette watched. The pink and purple color scheme she loved when her grandfather painted it now made her dizzy. It was becoming more and more obvious that she would have to go outside her church, as far outside as possible.

"You want me to do this for you, Angelica? I don't think you're going to be able to do it."

Angelica didn't answer. Jeanette was beginning to annoy her. She flipped the pages of her book, her eyes coming to rest on other names, checking off those that had any association with the church. Jeanette watched as she dialed a few more numbers, most of which went unanswered or were changed. She sat on the floor and grabbed the remote for Angelica's small television. She cruised through a few more channels with the television on mute and stopped at BET.

A music video silently flickered on the set. A nightclub scene caught Angelica's eye. She strode over and turned up the volume. Destiny's Child gyrated on the screen as lights flashed around them. "Ladies, leave your man at home!" Why hadn't she thought of this first?

"This is it! I should have thought of this before. The obvious place to meet a man who wants no strings attached is the club!" She danced around the room pointing at the TV.

"Uh, you can't dance, remember? And I thought you didn't like the club all that much. You might need me to go, at least to get you dressed up for the part, right?"

"I think not." Angelica shook her head. "I'll be okay." She knew Jeanette meant well, but her outfits were a little on the wild side and they didn't always match. Not to her liking anyway. "I love you, but you are the worst dresser since Lisa Bonet on the *Cosby Show* reruns. I can really handle it."

"I don't know why you had to go there. You just lack my sense of style. You handle your business."

Angelica had work to do. When Jeanette left, she started right away on her new game plan.

9

Juan started up his delivery truck and prepared to make his final deliveries of the day. He was still full of energy and caffeine. He enjoyed the solitude that driving the delivery truck gave him. It allowed him time to think. Juan definitely preferred driving the truck to staying in the office and listening to James. That man could gab. And he was forever in Juan's business. Other people's business was almost a part-time job for him, especially when it came to Sabrina.

No doubt Sabrina was finer than a Michael Jordan finger roll. Period. That could not be taken away from her, no matter what she did.

It wasn't like Juan didn't try. He wined and dined her and did everything his pops wanted him to. Sabrina was handpicked for him. Almost like old-fashioned arranged hookup, except she wasn't really Latina. Sabrina was a bona fide New York–type mixture. Her mother was Trinidadian and her father was Puerto Rican one generation re-moved. Her grandfather had lived near Juan's grandfather back in Puerto Rico when they were children, and their families refound each other in the Bronx. That made her Caribbean enough for his parents. They would have loved it if he and Sabrina could have gotten together. Damn, they would have made beautiful smart babies, too. But Juan wasn't feeling it.

Sabrina appeared to like him well enough. They had dated for two years. She thought he was a catch. She told his sister that, but she didn't love him. Juan could feel that in his heart.

He didn't trust her from day one. And he was glad he didn't. His instincts were always right. Juan still believed he would know his true love when he saw her. And he never saw her in Sabrina.

Most guys would have lost their cool when they walked into the scene Juan had walked into. But not him. His nostrils flared as he thought about it. He should have been angry, but he had just felt humiliated. The whole thing just confirmed what he already knew. Juan laughed. James had no idea how cool his head had really been.

He remembered the day clearly. He'd been out at the bas-ketball court when he got hurt playing ball. He knew she would be at her place making him a special dinner. He smiled at the thought. Saturday night was always their spe-cial date night. She would spend all day preparing some of her homemade Trini-rican specialties.

He hoped she was making him some roti. He absolutely

loved her cooking, even if he didn't love her. That girl knew her way around the kitchen. Like a trained gourmet cook, she mastered dishes from seven islands plus the good old United States. It was as if she had ancestors from each and every place. This was one of the things that made her wife material, at least according to his father.

But Juan didn't smell any cooking as he limped to her apartment that day. He put the key in the lock. No pots were banging. Things were so out of place he could smell it. The only thing missing was an eerie sound track like in the movies.

He opened the door and could hear sounds that shouldn't be coming from the living room, at least not without him in it. Sabrina was getting busy in there like she wasn't even expecting him, with some guy he'd never seen before. Juan was speechless as he was confronted with Sabrina, on the couch, legs spread wide, head back in ecstasy. The guy was there with her on the floor, on his knees, his head between her legs. Love funk everywhere. Damn! His girl. And he was at her place so much he practically lived there.

Juan watched and blinked, but he felt nothing he was supposed to feel. No anger. No sadness. Just insulted. Finally, he cleared his throat.

"Ahem."

They continued. He cleared his throat louder.

"Ahem."

Sabrina jumped up, attempting to cover herself. Her partner barely possessed the decency to use the back of his hand to wipe his face. He grinned at Juan and spat in the ashtray.

"Juan! How long have you been here?" Her voice had that high-pitched quality that told him she was about to lie. No lying necessary here. He saw what he saw. He turned toward the door.

"But, let me explain!"

"Not necessary. Don't say anything. I'll just leave. You are obviously busy."

"It just happened!"

Now, that was lame. "Uh-huh. Is he the grocery delivery boy or what? Did he trip and fall that way? I'm out of here."

Juan walked into the bathroom and closed the door to collect the few things he kept at her house. When he came out, the two of them were gone. He removed her key from his key ring and put it on the counter in plain sight. Good thing he found out before he asked her to get married. He knew then that pleasing his father was not going to be the best thing for him. He could be miserable if he kept trying to live his life that way. Juan needed to do more of what he wanted instead.

Sabrina had attempted to call him several times after that, but he'd refused her calls. He didn't want an explanation from her. He didn't want anything from her. That was two months ago. He wished her well.

Perhaps this trip to Baton Rouge was a good thing, a chance to get away. He hadn't told James about what had happened in his living room that day. Just said they'd broken up. He felt like a fool. Played. He knew full well that

Sabrina didn't just trip and fall and end up in bed with that guy. Something led her there. And from the looks of the way they were going about it, it had been leading there quite a while. With him the only one not knowing. He was the one walking around looking like a fool.

He rubbed his eyes, hoping to run across another Starbucks before the night was out. Might as well have stock in the place; he must have stopped in about five or six times today. He would be high on caffeine for a while, with as much java as he had consumed today. He'd tried almost every one of the specialty drinks on the menu. He almost couldn't get all the deliveries done for running to the bathroom.

Juan glanced at his list. He had just one more delivery. And then he could get some sleep.

10

Angelica studied for six hours. There was not much room for mistakes. She watched the Lifetime channel, BET, and MTV. She read everything from Joan Collins to Eric Jerome Dickey. She even reviewed *Mademoiselle* and *The Single Girl's Guide to Hunting and Fishing*. Angelica wanted to get it right, make sure she would say the right things. Her outfit was carefully picked, virtually from the pages of *Sista-Girl* magazine. She wanted to be sure to straddle the line between hoochie-mama and vamp. Every man in the club had to want her. Had to think it was his idea. Angelica wanted them to be crazy for her. She wanted to take her pick, and once it was over, she would be through with him.

Her dress was a short leopard print. A form-fitting number with a scoop neck. Painted on. On her feet she wore knee-high boots with an almost three-inch heel. Angelica pulled them on and smiled; they covered up her ankles.

Her grandfather used to say she had "Petersburg ankles," so called because they were skinny, like the girls he met in Petersburg, Virginia, as a young man. Might as well accentuate her positives. Small waist. Legs to her ears. Hair beaten into submission with a hint of wildness to it. Her outfit highlighted her best features and a Victoria's Secret Miracle Bra did the rest.

She looked into the mirror to put the finishing touches on her hair and makeup. But instead of seeing her own face, Angelica stared into the misty gray eyes of her grandfather. She gasped and blinked. He was still there. Her lips curled into a smile. She half imagined and half remembered him and a warm feeling came over her. He smiled at her as he had done so many times, his head covered with the same curly black hair. Even in her memory, the streak of shocking gray that had electrified his looks since he was twenty years old still lent a handsomeness to his face.

"Angelica-girl, you sure look fine."

Angelica felt tears sting her eyes. "You're going to make me ruin my makeup, Pop-pop. Why do you want me to do this?" She dabbed at her eyes with a tissue and tried to keep her mascara from running.

"The only thing I want you to do is what you think is right."

Angelica licked her lips to moisten them and glanced back into the mirror. The only face she now saw was hers. She didn't fully understand her grandfather's request, but he always seemed to know what he was doing. She glanced at her watch and sighed as she grabbed her car keys.

Angelica knew she could only get what she needed if the effect was *puh-dow!* Taking one last glance in the mirror, she knew it was. She licked her finger and smoothed her one lock that always strayed out of place. Her shoulder-length hair perfectly framed her face and then led the eye to focus on her chest.

Her favorite piece of jewelry hung around her neck. For days, Angelica had not taken off the emerald and diamond brooch given to her by her grandfather. When he gave it to her for her twentieth birthday, she'd thought it was too large and too big to be worn by a woman her age. Now she thought it was perfect. The brooch seemed especially designed for her. It nestled at the top of the valley between her breasts, now made more attractive by her Miracle Bra. She stroked it like it was a good-luck charm.

Bakari was a relatively new club in town. Angelica had never been there, but she'd heard a lot about it. They hosted a lot of events in the community, trying to stir up business with the professionals in town. There was even free valet parking for ladies arriving alone.

Angelica blotted her lipstick and stepped out of her car. The valet parking attendant stared at her. She could not hold back her smile. The rapacious way he looked at her confirmed that her outfit was right on target.

She heard music coming from the club that she did not recognize. It was upbeat music and Angelica automatically changed her rhythm to match that of the music. Bakari featured a mixture of music. There was even a jazz room for the thirty-something crowd, the older set.

Angelica looked around at the mélange of brass and glass furniture and fixtures in the entryway. Nicely done. She hoped the patrons here would be above the scrubs and the holy rollers she knew. Angelica paused in front of the door and straightened her dress, tugging it down. She held her breath, realizing that the man at the door was expecting her to show her ID.

Damn! She hadn't thought about that. She whipped it out, placing her thumb over her birth date. The man smiled at her, and she smiled back. Maybe he would be too busy looking at her to notice her birth date. She was so close to being of age anyway.

"Welcome to Bakari. First time?"

Angelica nodded as he attempted to take her driver's license from her. They tugged it back and forth for a while.

"You have to let it go, honey. I have to scan it." He wrenched the card from her hand.

"Oh, high-tech, huh?" Angelica batted her eyes and smiled, laughing nervously. She watched as he ran it through a scanner, like in the grocery store. The screen blinked red.

Angelica's heart sank. She had not considered that she might not be able to get into the club.

"Oh, miss, you aren't quite twenty-one yet, huh?"

"But I will be in six days!" Angelica fought back the tears that threatened to spring from her flawlessly made-up eyes.

"That's okay, sweetie, the law is the law. You have to

wear a bracelet, and you will not be able to drink. You also have to pay the cover charge. That will be ten dollars. Have a good time." As he spoke, he grabbed her right arm and affixed a yellow plastic bracelet. Angelica handed over the money, breathing a sigh of relief. In was in, and that was the point, right? She stepped through the door and into her inheritance.

Bakari was just as tastefully furnished on the inside as it had been in the reception area. Angelica looked around, relieved. She mostly avoided the clubs that served underage people because they tended to be holes-in-the-wall, seedy. It seemed they all served fried catfish, too, so when you left, you smelled like cigarette smoke and fish. Bakari had polished wood floors with state-of-the-art lighting. The large dance floor was rimmed by tables—and not the folding kind—covered with real tablecloths. Most had small centerpieces of fresh flowers in the center. Angelica inhaled and smiled a little. She could not detect any fish.

Most of the crowd looked to be at least three or four years older than Angelica. She found a table where she could see the dance floor well. The bracelet on her arm made her suddenly lose her confidence. She pushed it under her sleeve so that no one could tell she was underage. But if they knew the kind of money she was about to inherit, her age would not matter. She knew that.

Angelica smiled and ordered a Shirley Temple from the waitress. No use making the wrong kind of scene. She wanted all eyes on her because she was irresistible, not because the waitress was laughing at her for trying to order an alcoholic drink. Angelica had not learned to like the taste of alcohol yet anyway, so she knew she wouldn't miss it. There was no drinking in her Pop-pop's house. He firmly believed that the only thing a person should be high on was life. Not that he wasn't a hell-raiser back in the day; he'd shared more than one story with Angelica about how he was a cutup in his younger days.

A few people started dancing and Angelica tapped her foot under the table along with the beat. She surveyed the room, checking out the possibilities. She wanted to make sure to pick someone who would say yes to her proposition. Deep in her thoughts and her planning, she felt a tap on her shoulder. Angelica turned around to face a tall, handsome man. She let her eyes gallop freely, checking him out. His pale, yellow-brown skin was flawless, his mouth framed by a perfectly sculpted mustache and goatee. He was fine-featured, and he smiled, exposing near-perfect teeth. Not bad.

"Dance?" He motioned toward the dance floor and Angelica stood up to follow. From behind, he didn't look bad, at least better than any of the behinds Angelica saw in church. On the dance floor, he smiled at her, and Angelica noted that he was not bad-looking at all. His skin was perfect, and he sported an almost dimple when he smiled. Medium build, twisted hair. Sophisticated and well dressed. Smelled good, too. A good sign. Not gorgeous, but handsome, sexy. He would do. Angelica caught herself; Pop-pop didn't say anything about falling in love or getting married, he just wanted her to do the deed.

They danced for two songs, and Angelica tried to dance as sexily as she possibly could, like the women in the music videos. She wanted one thing and one thing only on his mind. Her partner licked his lips, obviously checking her out. From the look on his face, she knew she was succeeding in getting him interested. There would be no mere kisses on the forehead tonight.

"My name is Jeffrey." He leaned into her, talking above the music.

Angelica smiled, batting her eyelashes. "Angelica," she said. "Would you like to sit?" She felt her palms sweating and rubbed her hands together quickly. The ball was set in motion.

He nodded, and this time Angelica led. She found the jazz room. Angelica was not really fond of jazz, but it was much quieter than in the main room. It would be a hell of a lot easier to get to first base if they could hear each other talk.

"You come here a lot?"

Angelica frowned. Why did he have to start with that line? "No, you?"

"Actually this is my first time here. I thought I would check it out. Some of the guys at the office have been here several times already."

"Office?" It wouldn't hurt to know what he did for a living.

"I am a software engineer." He looked at her, squinting. "You know, you look real familiar."

"I don't think so." At least he was intelligent. She didn't

want to add that she was a funeral home heiress. Might as well cut to the chase. "Boy, I'm hungry. Want to go eat?"

For a minute, Angelica saw a quick look of surprise come over Jeffrey's face. He recovered fast.

"Uh, yeah. I guess I am a little hungry. Where do you want to go?"

Angelica had thought this out before she left home, carefully planning what she was going to say and do when given the chance.

"How about your place? You cook, don't you? You certainly don't look like you're starving." She licked her finger for accent. Angelica watched as Jeffrey coughed, nearly choking on his drink.

"No can do, Miss Angelica. I am temporarily living with my mother."

That moved him down several notches on the "good catch" list. No matter, she didn't need to stay in touch.

Jeffrey moved in very close to Angelica and licked her ear. Angelica could tell that the possibilities were beginning to excite him, but she was annoyed. He looked way too old to still be living with his mother. These were not normal times and one day of the six Angelica had was almost gone.

She'd planned for mishaps, and switched to plan B. "Oh. Well, then, how about the Hilton? We could go there. I heard they have a fabulous restaurant there, and they're open late."

The Hilton was out of the way, near the airport. And if they ate at a hotel, it would be easy to just go get a room.

Angelica was on a mission and the only bush she wanted to beat around tonight was hers.

"So do you want to follow me?" he asked.

Angelica had thought about this, too. She didn't get any bad vibes from Jeffrey, so she felt comfortable riding with him. Although the hotel was out of the way, she didn't want to take a chance on anyone seeing her car parked in its parking lot.

"I'll ride with you. You can bring me back here to pick up my car, okay?"

Jeffrey wiped his face with his hand and swallowed hard. He noticed that he was sweating, and a smile crept over his face. This was going to be his lucky night.

The ride to the hotel was almost silent, the longest twenty minutes Angelica had ever experienced. They both held their breath the entire way. Jeffrey's car was reasonably clean, but the air inside was thick with cheap air freshener. Angelica wanted to open the window but did not dare; she didn't want to insult him before they even got started.

They listened to the radio and Angelica could not help but think how mad her grandfather would be with her for riding with this stranger. She could hear him like he was right next to her, warning her about driving with strangers and making sure she was in control of getting where she needed to be at all times. He wanted her to always make sure she had a way home.

The more she thought about it, the more surprised she became about his unusual requirement that he wanted her to fulfill to get her inheritance. Her Pop-pop always had his reasons for the things he did while he was alive, so he probably had them in his death, too. She hoped that this all would eventually make sense.

They finally pulled into the parking lot. Angelica glanced at her watch. It was still early, barely ten o'clock. She looked around, suddenly realizing that the parking lot was fuller than she imagined it would be. This was not good.

"You okay?" Jeffrey had already made his way around the car to open her door.

"Fine. Let's go." Angelica gulped and took the hand he offered. She hoped he wouldn't notice her sweaty hands. She fingered the condoms she'd stashed in her jacket pocket. Pop-pop said get laid, not get a disease.

They entered the hotel through the main lobby, and Angelica looked around. For ten o'clock at night, the lobby seemed to be very full of people, mainly women. Angelica noticed that they were all wearing some kind of a badge. She couldn't read it, but she saw enough to realize she had walked smack into the middle of a convention.

She tugged at Jeffrey's hand. Angelica did not want to risk being seen by anyone. "Hey, do you think we could order room service instead of eating in the restaurant?"

"R-r-room service?" He stuttered.

What a dimwit, she thought. Can't he tell when a girl is about to give it up? She batted her eyelids and leaned into him. Jeffrey recovered from his blank moment. "Okay, yeah, "he said, "I'll get a room."

"And I'll go to the bathroom. Meet me by the elevators."

Angelica walked toward the restroom, her heels clicking on the floor. She brushed past a woman who was in her path and looked at the floor, not wanting to make eye contact with any of the people milling about the lobby. They might guess what she was doing at the hotel, or question her, and she knew she was not prepared to answer any questions. She just wanted to get this whole thing over with so she could get on with her life.

By the time she got back to the elevators, Jeffrey was there waiting for her. Angelica almost felt sorry for him as she took in the silly-looking grin on his face. Is this what men did to women? she wondered. Is this how they plotted and schemed when they wanted to get into someone's panties?

The woman from the bathroom walked past the bank of elevators as the doors opened. Angelica looked down at the floor and grabbed Jeffrey's hand, pulling him into the elevator. She was terrified—for a moment the woman reminded her of Sister Ruby, the choir director at her church. She slammed her finger on the button to close the doors.

"What floor?" She was relieved that Jeffrey did not seem to notice her reaction. He seemed to merely think she was eager. He was certainly full of himself.

"Six."

They rode to the sixth floor in silence. When they left the elevator, Angelica followed Jeffrey without talking. She stared at the stains on the carpet as they walked to their room at the end of the hall. She waited patiently as Jeffrey opened the door with the card key.

Jeffrey seemed to have gotten over his shock. He strode into the room confidently, going straight to the minibar.

"Should I order some wine before dinner?"

Angelica plopped into a chair, grabbing the television remote.

"Wine would be nice." She was going to need all the fortification she could get.

"You don't mind if I take off my shoes, do ya?"

"No, baby, take off anything you want," she said.

He laughed. "Never say anything I want, I might take you up on that."

He removed his jacket and ordered wine from room service. He really wasn't bad-looking in the light. Angelica admired the way his hair was styled in pre-dreadlock twists. Well-groomed locks on a good-looking man. Sexy. It was her turn to wet her lips, and then she caught herself. She didn't need to be getting attached.

"Weren't you afraid to come up here with me? I could be a serial killer or something, you know."

"But you're not. My instincts told me you were a good person. Besides, serial killers are almost always white males. I saw that on television."

"Do you believe everything you see on TV? You should still be careful. The world is full of crazies. I'm sure you know that." He moved closer to where Angelica was now standing. She turned around to face him and noticed they were suddenly very close.

"Yeah, I know that, but I got good vibes from you. I always trust my instincts."

He moved forward and placed the softest lips Angelica had ever felt onto hers, kissing her gently. He deftly parted her lips with his tongue, probing her mouth. Angelica felt her body respond, her mouth following his lead. He was good!

"Well, you should be more careful. I am not a serial killer or anything, but I sure felt like a degenerate around all those church women downstairs. There must be a conference here or something."

Angelica felt her body stiffen. How did he know they were church women? She realized that she was holding her breath.

"You know, for a minute I even thought I recognized someone from the new church I've been going to. This woman named Ruby was really nice to me when I first came. Made me feel at home."

Angelica choked on her own saliva. The clock stopped in the room. She stepped back and smoothed her dress. What was she thinking? Of all the people in the club, how could she possibly pick up someone who went to the same church?

Angelica was out the door faster than Jeffrey could say amen. With her boots in her hand, she hopped into the elevator. She pressed the lobby floor button frantically, willing it to close before she was followed. She slipped her feet into her boots during the descent to the first floor, swearing under her breath during the trip. The elevator could not descend fast enough. How could she have been so stupid? It was a good thing he'd said something, or she might have had all the saints in the church in her business. The rest of her time in Baton Rouge would be a living hell.

Although the lobby was still filled with activity, the click of Angelica's three-inch heels seemed to thunder across the lobby. The shoes felt silly now and Angelica expected to fall forward on her face any minute. She focused on the revolving door that would lead her to freedom and almost sprinted. Relaxing as she finally reached the door, Angelica released the breath she was holding since she left the room. The night was a waste. She stepped into the revolving door and looked up as it slowed. Her world began to move in slow motion. A young man stepped into the door from the other side.

Through the glass of the doors, Angelica could see he was dressed in some type of uniform, with a company label on his left shoulder, and he was struggling with a load of dry cleaning. The shirt hugged the curves of his muscled chest like it was his hide instead of his clothing. He was gorgeous! Time was standing still again, but for a different reason. All of Angelica's senses seemed to be frozen and everything else, all sight, all sound, all smell, was momentarily blocked. For a split second, there was no convention in the lobby, and getting away from Jeffrey momentarily left her mind. Here was the most gorgeous man she had ever seen. He was glowing all over. His face was cocoa-brown, and he had curly brown hair. High cheek-bones and sultry brown eyes highlighted by perfect eye-lashes. He had his own personal halo and only Angelica could see it.

Angelica was so busy basking in the glow emanating from this person that when she stepped back into the lobby, she almost fell. Instead of exiting, she'd walked in a complete circle. The lights and activity in the hotel lobby jarred her back into consciousness. Information from her senses rushed at her from all directions at once. Her mouth was still open. She stood still and watched as the man who had stopped her world walked over to the lobby counter. She followed him with her eyes, simultaneously fighting the flood of information rushing toward her.

"Angelica! What happened?" She saw Jeffrey striding toward her. Angelica panicked, turning on her heels. She jumped back into the revolving door. There was a cab on the other side, and Angelica snatched its door. She jumped in, taking her wallet out of her purse.

"I'm off duty," the cabdriver said.

"Well, why the hell are you sitting here?"

"Off duty, ma'am."

Angelica grabbed her things in a panic. Jeffrey was nearing the hotel door. She exited the cab through the other side and ran across the street to the bus stop. She tried to blend in with the small crowd of people there. She said a quick prayer under her breath and the cab pulled off. Jeffrey was now standing on the curb in front of the hotel with his shirt still open.

Angelica started to sweat. She had no idea what she was going to say to him. At that moment, a bus pulled in. Angelica opened her bag and fished for one of her bus tokens. She breathed a sigh of relief. It sure was a good thing Pop-

pop always made her keep spare tokens. Her prayers seemed to be answered. The ride home would give her more time to formulate a new plan. One that would work next time. She could go get her car tomorrow.

She could have made a big mistake. Her heart pounded in her ears. She thought she could get this done very quickly, but now she knew it was going to be harder than she ever imagined. Angelica let her head rest against the bus window. Did it happen this way with guys, too? She wondered. It certainly didn't look that hard.

11

Thirty-two deliveries in one night. Juan wiped the sweat from his forehead with the back of his hand. He was starting to see double. He was finally at the end of his delivery list and he was glad. It must have taken him twice as long as it should have, with James calling him every other minute to make sure he was delivering the right robes to the right places.

Juan couldn't deny that he had been entertained the whole night, at least during his stops. At every delivery, it was the same thing. Black folks, lots of them, dressed from head to toe in their finest, even though they were going to put robes over their clothes. Suits of every color imaginable, and out-of-this-world hats, of every shape, size and color. Juan smiled as he thought about it. Sunday best, even though it wasn't Sunday.

As he walked in and out of the hotels, Juan was reassured of his sexual appeal. More than one of the sisters, and a couple of the brothers, had propositioned him. Church-going or not, Juan knew that none of the women, no matter how finely they were dressed, were for him. He knew, deep down, that the woman for him would have a beauty that came from within. He didn't want to be the fool again.

He glanced at his list. His last delivery for the night was to the Hilton, out near the airport. Juan remembered seeing it as he left the airport when he arrived from New York. Its distance from everything else was the main reason he'd left it for last. All he had to do was drop off the robes at the desk.

James's voice came over the radio. "Juan? You there?"

"Where else would I be? What's up?"

"Nothing, I was just checking on ya, that's all."

"James, man, you know I got it all under control. I printed out all the directions for my entire night before I left. That, combined with your three-page list—man, I'm straight."

"They're waiting for you at the Hilton. They can't go to sleep until they're sure they have their robes for tomorrow. The woman called the office three times."

"Did you tell her that the Delgado Brothers never disappoint? She needs to hold her horses! I'll tell her myself when I see her." Juan smiled.

"Ah, you better hold your tongue. Knowing you, you'll turn on the charm as soon as you see her. Listen, we are on for tomorrow. We have to go down to the spot so you can meet the club manager. He is anxious to hear a sample of your sweet sax playing."

"A'right. I'm ready for that. Too bad he ain't a *she*. I could make him melt in no time flat. With a single note."

"Juan, your head is going to be too big for the truck, Jefe."

"You're just jealous. Anyway, I'm at the Hilton now. Later, man."

Juan positioned the mike back in its cradle and stopped the delivery truck in the Hilton parking lot. He immediately noticed all the cars still in the lot and double-checked his delivery instructions. The purple robes he was delivering all belonged to a church called Mt. Moriah Church of the Lost Pilgrim. What kind of a name was that? He walked around to the back of the truck and lifted the gate. There sure seemed to be a lot of lost pilgrims; there were over a hundred robes in this bunch. He would have to make several trips.

Juan made his way across the parking lot and struggled to keep from tripping on the dry-cleaning plastic. He was carrying so many robes at one time that he could barely see where he was going. The robes slid against one another, and Juan automatically juggled them around to keep from losing any. His mind kept wandering; he was trying to compose the few bars of music to play tomorrow night at his audition. James assured him that it was in the bag; his cousin owned the club. But Juan didn't want to take anything for granted. He wanted to be as good as possible.

Juan made it to the Hilton door without losing any robes. He juggled them one more time, his hands aching from holding onto the slippery plastic. He paused in front of the revolving door to grab all of the robes by the hangers. No use in having customers thinking he was delivering wrinkled or mistreated merchandise.

Struggling to grasp all of the hangers, he stepped into the revolving door. They began to cut into his fingers as he entered the lobby. He held them as steadily as possible and hurriedly walked over to the front desk. Luckily, an empty bellman's cart was nearby. Without even asking, he immediately hung first the robes he held in his right hand, and then those in his left. He stretched his fingers, quickly mimicking fingering his saxophone, and he felt the blood start to flow through them again.

"I'm looking for the manager." He talked over the counter to no one in particular. This hotel lobby was no different from the others he had seen tonight. It was larger and there seemed to be a lot more activity. People were everywhere, all still dressed in their finest clothes and wearing gold convention name tags. Unlike the others, this hotel seemed to be the center of the action.

"I'll be right with you, sir."

Juan turned back around to the desk. He couldn't tell who spoke. Everyone seemed to have gone back to whatever task they were originally doing when he walked up.

"I have more outside. I'll be back." Juan started back toward the door, his head down.

A guy with an open shirt walked, almost ran, in front of Juan, cutting him off. "Angelica! What happened?" He shouted.

Juan stepped back and shook his head. The man didn't

even say excuse me. And they say New Yorkers are rude! *Cabrón!*

He watched the open-shirted fellow go through the revolving door in front of him. By the time Juan came through the door, the guy closed his shirt and was standing in the portico, looking around. His hands were on his hips.

"Hey, man, did you see a woman come through the lobby before me?"

"Naw, I'm sorry."

"Pretty girl? Young?"

The brother looked dejected and Juan instantly knew he wanted no part of whatever his particular drama was. He had been there himself, all too recently. Juan shook his head and tugged on the fold at the bottom of his shirt, smoothing it.

The man looked sad in the way only a woman could make a man look. Juan headed toward the truck for the second part of his delivery. The long day was catching up with him and all he wanted to do was sleep.

12

Deborah was used to being the belle of the ball. She worked hard at it and saw no reason why she couldn't do the same for this conference. Her husband's church was coordinating the largest gospel convention and concert ever. Deborah checked her reflection in the doors one last time before she walked into the hotel lobby. Perfect was still perfect. She was on a mission and was determined to do her best to look the part of a woman almost thirty years younger than her well-respected husband. She glanced over at her daughter Ché, who appeared to be in the middle of some kind of weird dance. She twitched and carried on something terrible.

"What are you doing, girl?" Deborah narrowed her eyes. Ché was always embarrassing her. Why hadn't she learned how to look the part of First Family yet?

"I'm fixing my dang slip, Ma. It is riding up under my dress and we just barely got here." Ché fidgeted some more and moved in a way that reminded Deborah of someone who'd stepped in a bed of red ants.

"If you keep that up, folks will think you have some kinda disease. Just hold your head up and walk right. Act like you're creating a new style."

"I hate these things. A man must have invented them. I am going to take it off the first chance I get."

They walked through the revolving door into the hotel lobby. It was full of life. The convention seemed to be in full swing and the opening session wasn't scheduled for another forty minutes.

They were greeted with "Hello, Mrs. Davis" from several different directions. Ché glanced over at her mother, who had a phony smile plastered to her face. Another minute and she would surely do the beauty pageant wave.

"Just follow my lead, okay?" Deborah smiled and nodded at the women bustling through the lobby, glancing at her daughter only briefly. Deborah did not dare look at her daughter too long. Deep in her heart, she knew that there was no way Ché could even partially look like she was at home in the midst of all this activity, no matter how hard Deborah had worked with her. This was Deborah's world, not hers. Deborah only had to put up with her for two more years, and then she would be eighteen. She would be done with her then.

"Ma, I need to go to the bathroom." Ché lurched forward once more, this time with a new twist of her hips, in hopes of putting her slip back in place.

"You fix that thing, but don't take it off, you hear? You

need to be grateful that we can afford to get you the proper undergarments. You know they are crucial for a lady." Deborah continued to nod at the people passing her, talking at Ché through her teeth without moving her lips.

Ché sucked her teeth and headed for the bathroom, her mother following without looking like there was any urgency about her at all. No one would know she concerned herself with such trivial things as her daughter's undergarments.

"You know, I can't tell that there is anything at all wrong with your slip. You sure there is a problem?"

"Ma, how can you possibly take in everything that is going on around you and still manage to check out my butt?" Ché knew that she could be standing perfectly beauty-queen still and her mother would still find something to pick at. She pushed open the bathroom door and was barely able to step inside the room. There was a line of women, all wearing tags from the conference.

Deborah went into a stall first. Ché waited as patiently as possible, looking into the mirror while she waited. She spread her generous lips and checked her teeth in the mirror. The line moved fast, and she felt someone watching her from the end of it. She turned her head back toward the door and smiled, trying to give her very best "Deborah" smile.

"Well, if it isn't Ché Davis. How are you, baby?" Sister Ruby greeted her the way she greeted every young woman in the church. Her singsong voice was almost lost in the general buzz of conversation in the crowded bathroom.

"I'm fine, ma'am. How are you?" Ché did not want to make conversation. Deborah stepped from the stall, saving her. She took over the conversation as always, and Ché slipped inside the stall without so much as a good-bye. She removed her slip carefully and placed it in her purse. What her mother didn't know wouldn't hurt her. She should have followed her instincts and not put the slip on in the first place. Her mother spent so many years conning people that she was always too concerned with appearances and making things look right. Ché listened halfheartedly at the chatter outside her stall, attempting to look over her shoulder at her well-rounded behind. She knew her mother would not be able to tell that she was slipless.

Ché could hear her mother and Sister Ruby outside the stall. She followed their voices as they left the bathroom, forgetting about her and stepping into the hallway. The closing door of the bathroom cut off their conversation. Ché made her way to the sink. Although she had not used the bathroom, she felt obligated to wash her hands. Ché made a face at herself in the mirror; she was much more like her mother than she wanted to be, but she still didn't want the other sisters in the room thinking she was nasty because they did not see her wash her hands. She finished and reached for a towel. She looked up and glimpsed someone who looked like Angelica Chappee leaving the restroom. Now, she was the last person that Ché expected to see at the conference. The choir wasn't singing until tomorrow, and although Angelica did sing with the choir on occasion, she wasn't expected to here, and not for a while anyway, since her grandfather had just died.

Ché dried her hands and hurried through the door. There was no sight of her mother. The Angelica look-alike jumped onto the elevator. Ché wanted to say a quick hello, get that friendship going that her mother had mandated. She started toward the elevator bank, only to see the doors close before she could get there.

Well, well, Ché thought. Her prayers were answered. If that really was Angelica, she certainly did not look like she was dressed for any church function. And was there a man in there with her? That could only mean one thing. Ché smiled. Now, that bit of information was something she could use to her advantage. It would be much easier than pretending to make friends, anyway, and much more fun.

13

Jeanette's house was closer. Angelica held her breath and she scurried through the dark neighborhood. The neighborhood consisted of middle-class and well-kept row houses built in the 1940s. Small patches of lawn interspersed the concrete sidewalks and driveways. The houses were close enough together that it would not be too hard to look inside a neighbor's house from inside your own if you tried, but no one ever did.

All of the streetlights seemed to be out and the only sound on the street was that of an occasional car passing by. Angelica could not help looking over her shoulder every few feet. She paused in front of her friend's small house; the light that shone through the windows made the house seem sinister, like it was laughing at her and the disaster the evening had become.

It would be no good to disturb Jeanette's parents. Angelica did not want to hear them pity her or look at her as if she had gone crazy for being out so late. Despite what she said, Jeanette was hardly ever allowed out past midnight. Like Angelica's grandfather, Jeanette's parents insisted that as long as Jeanette lived in their house, she had to live by their rules.

Angelica skirted the lawn and made her way to the back of the house. She could hear the neighbor's dog barking and hoped it would stay wherever it was and not come running out at her. Her feet were killing her as it was—her boots had seen better days—and she did not think she had the energy to sprint down the block with a dog chasing her.

Jeanette's window was open. Angelica only had to call Jeanette once before she appeared at the window, rubbing her eyes.

Jeanette's head was tied up with a purple silk scarf, with three large pink sponge rollers on top. Her face was bare and she squinted as she stuck her head out of the window.

"I ain't even gonna ask you what you are doing here." She yawned. "Did you do it? I know there is a good reason for you to be at my window. You know how I am about my beauty sleep."

"Where are your glasses? Can I come in? And can we not discuss it?" Angelica removed her boots and hiked her dress. She threw the boots through the window and shimmied through it after them.

"What would you do if I lived on the second floor?" Jeanette asked.

"I would probably learn how to climb a tree." Angelica paused so her eyes could adjust to the light Jeanette had turned on.

The room was small and painted bright yellow. It had been added onto the house some years ago behind the kitchen and was the only bedroom on the ground floor. Jeanette had two identical beds in her room, twin-sized, and one small nightstand, and the room smelled of Jeanette's woodsy perfume. She flopped back down into her bed and Angelica sat on the other.

"Let me guess." Jeanette pulled the covers over her head as she spoke. "You couldn't do it."

"You don't seem surprised. I am such a dummy. I did meet a guy in the club. That wasn't a problem. Everything was going fine. But we ended up at the Hilton—"

"Where the church conference is going on."

"Well, if you knew that, why didn't you tell me? Do you have something I can sleep in?" Angelica stood up and moved the two steps across the small room. She began to rifle through Jeanette's drawers.

"Check the top drawer. And you didn't ask. If you're going to be involved in these clandestine operations, I thought you'd do your homework. And you said you didn't need help, remember? You know how you get."

Angelica peeled her dress off and dropped it onto the floor. She pulled a large T-shirt over her head. "This ain't no spy or crime movie. I can't think of everything."

"I didn't say you could. Can I get to sleep now?" She turned her back to Angelica and pulled the covers farther up around her neck.

"Are you saying I'm incapable? You don't think I can do this, is that it?"

"Look, Angelica, I am not saying that you're Miss Goody Two Shoes or that you can't get this done, it's just that you always do what you want anyway, right? You have always been that way. Do you remember when we were about seven years old, and your grandparents told you not to cross the street, but you wanted to go to the candy store? I told you not to go 'cause you were going to get in trouble. What did you do?"

Angelica's face softened. "I convinced you to go with me and we went to the candy store anyway, crossing the street and all."

"And what did you tell your grandfather when he asked why you disobeyed him? You told him that your grandma told you to always think about what you wanted and decide whether you can accept the consequences for your actions—"

"And I decided that I could accept the punishment because I *really* wanted some Jolly Rancher candy."

"That's right. So I see no reason to help you if you have already told me that you don't want my help. You need to figure out what you want to do and then find a way to do it. You're going to do that anyway, with or without my help. I'll be here when you're done."

Angelica paused. Maybe she *was* being too hasty. She slipped into bed. "Well, I need to add at least one other preliminary question to my checklist."

"Tell me about it in the morning, okay?"

Angelica nodded and closed her eyes. She was going to make sure she asked what church the guy attended before she tried to get him into bed. No more church boys if she could help it. One of her precious days was gone; she could not afford to lose any more.

By morning, it was no less unbelievable to Angelica what her grandfather wanted her to do to get her inheritance. She'd dreamed about him; he told her more than once that there was no need to buy the cow if you could get the milk for free. Maybe she was missing something.

She got up early, before Jeanette's parents, and made her way back to her own house. As she approached it, it even looked empty from the outside without Pop-pop there. She turned the key in the lock and could hear the phone ringing inside. She rushed in, smacking her lips. The foul taste in her mouth made her wish she had left a spare toothbrush at Jeanette's house. The clock next to the phone read nine A.M.

"Yeah?"

"Angelica? This is Damien Brown, returning your call."

She paused, remembering his number as one that was not answered when she called the night before.

"I saw your number on the caller ID. You called me, right? I was out of town. What have you been up to?"

She narrowed her eyes. "Nothing, really. I was just calling to see how you were doing. I was actually going to ask you to go to dinner with me yesterday. I felt like getting out."

"I see." Angelica could hear Damien breathing on the other end. "Well, look here. You still want to go? Since I wasn't here when you called, I can take *you*. I'm kinda surprised you called me. I never thought you would use the number when I gave it to you. You didn't seem that interested."

The plan to get her inheritance was not working well up to this point, and Angelica wasn't sure if Damien was the right person. She really didn't know too much about him. Maybe that made him perfect for the job.

She'd met Damien a few months before in the grocery store. He'd stopped behind her in the checkout line, flashing a smile so big, Angelica thought he was a little weird. His light brown eyes had opened wide when he grinned, and he sported an Afro that straddled the line between cool and being a sixties throwback. Someone obviously had told him that the grocery store was a good pickup spot; the only thing he was trying to purchase was a bottle of that new water with caffeine in it.

He'd told her then that he lived out of town, but came to Baton Rouge for business often. He said he kept a small apartment in town for those occasions. Seeing him in her mind, Angelica knew he was much older than she was, at least thirty, but he talked at her until she agreed to take his number just to get him to leave her alone.

"I didn't want you to think I was too eager! I ain't that kinda girl." She giggled. "Do you go to church?"

"Now, that's a strange question. I thought you wanted to go to dinner, not save my soul."

Angelica laughed. "Well, I do. I was just asking."

"I get it. This is the pre-date interrogation, huh? Is there a wrong answer? If I say the wrong thing, do I get the booby prize?"

"I was really just trying to make conversation. Besides, I am the booby prize." Angelica held her breath, not believing she had said that.

"I'm glad you called. And, just so you know, I wasn't really raised in a churchgoing family. But I don't really consider myself a heathen or anything. I hope that's okay."

Angelica felt herself smile. Juilliard was calling her. She glanced at her watch. "How's eight o'clock?"

After the first night's fiasco, Angelica decided it would be best to drive herself to her dates. It would make it easier for her to get away if she needed to. It was only the second day in her attempt and she was already feeling mentally tired. The idea of inheriting so much money was weighing on her mind. She knew it was her Pop-pop that put her in this predicament, but she wished he were there to talk to. Still, Angelica doubted she would be asking him to help her solve the problem of how to get a guy into bed. Even if she could ask him something like that, he would probably laugh at her and crack one of his *Reader's Digest* jokes. They would probably end up singing together like they often did. It was from him that Angelica inherited her love of music and her talent. She often told him he'd missed his calling when he went into the funeral home business. But after Grandma died, he wouldn't even sing in the choir.

She dressed more sensibly this time. The boots of last night were cute, but it had been hell getting them back on in the elevator. They were sexy without one ounce of practicality, definitely expiration-date boots, only good for a certain number of hours.

Angelica laughed to herself as she thought about how she must have looked flying from that hotel room. It reminded her of one of her grandfather's crazy stories, the ones he told about his escapades about growing up in Baltimore.

Tonight she opted for midheel pumps. They were pointed, and very sexy, but still easy to get on and off. She pulled on a short, swingy red skirt and looked in the mirror, humming as she dressed. The skirt fell softly over her butt, accentuating its curves and showing off her well-turned legs.

Just as she picked up her car keys, the phone rang. Angelica hoped it wasn't her date calling to cancel, and let the answering machine take it.

"Angelica, this is Ché, from Mt. Moriah, the pastor's daughter. I was calling to check on you and see how you were doing, find out if you needed anything. You can call me if you do, or if you just want to talk. I realize how difficult a time this must be for you. Anyway, I will understand if you don't call me." And she gave her number.

Angelica listened, raising one eyebrow. She and Ché were not exactly friends, but they weren't enemies, either. They attended the same church and occasionally some of the same church functions. She recalled that although she tried to be friendly on more than one occasion, Ché was mysterious and withdrawn since she arrived with her mother three years ago. No one knew much about her. Like most of the other folks in the church, Angelica suspected that Ché and her mother had some kind of a secret life somewhere, and her own set of friends.

Angelica recalled that Deborah tried to be friendly at first, almost too friendly. Her honeymoon was barely over before she was suggesting that Angelica and Pop-pop come to dinner with the pastor's new family. That ended quickly when Pop-pop wasn't interested. In fact, that was when he and the pastor stopped being so close. Angelica never was able to get out of him what their differences were really about. He just refused to discuss it. After that, neither Ché nor Deborah seemed too happy about having moved into town anymore. As time wore on, Deborah became very wary of the other people around them. At times she seemed almost paranoid and suspicious of everyone outside of the church social functions.

"You can't fault folks for that, baby girl," Pop-pop had said. "No one knows better than I do that sometimes it is best to just keep folks out of your business. And we are going to stay out of theirs, too." Angelica was cordial to both Ché and her mother, just as her grandfather suggested, but she thought they were being very strange. They continued to keep to themselves, not socializing much with the other church members.

They were part of the first family of the church, and they were under constant scrutiny, just like Grandpa had said. Everyone thought they knew their business no matter what they did, and seemed to be waiting for some major drama to occur or for them to leave town just as suddenly as they had arrived. Even Pop-pop held his breath every time someone mentioned Deborah's name. It was almost as if he knew something he refused to talk about. It was clear that some in the congregation resented their presence and wished them back where they had come from.

Angelica fiddled with her pantyhose and reset the answering machine. She had to admit that it was weird for the pastor to get such an instant family. There had been no prior mention of them and they just appeared one day, announced at a church service. Everyone was surprised; they had expected the pastor to remarry, but thought it would be one of the women from the congregation who were vying hard for his attention. Deborah was almost like a mail-order bride—too good to be true, she just popped up, on the surface, fitting the bill of Pastor's wife perfectly. Still, Angelica fleetingly wondered if Ché would be a good person to talk with, at least about how to get some males interested. If nothing else, Ché seemed to react best to the men in the church, at least better than Angelica did, and they all seemed to like Ché, too. She just could not develop a relationship with any of the young women, not even Jeanette, and Jeanette was friendly to everyone, even if they weren't friendly to her.

Angelica had agreed to meet Damien at a small café downtown. It was out of the way, on a street so narrow Angelica wondered if large cars could even pass through it. It wasn't a bad place for its location. It stood almost at the end of the street, almost by itself. The neighboring businesses appeared to be empty, or at least daytime-only type establishments.

The entrance was almost unmarked, except for a little hand-painted sign that read TWO STEPS DOWN. Angelica hesitated before walking down the two steps, for which the place was appropriately named, to the entrance. Feeling like she had stepped into an old-fashioned speakeasy, she was greeted by the smell of warm beignets mixed with the aroma of coffee.

The room was hazy and filled with cigarette and cigar smoke. After her eyes adjusted to the dim light, she felt more comfortable and at home. Two Steps Down was nicely furnished, in a bistro style. The light fixtures were reminiscent of old-fashioned gaslights, with the flame replaced by tiny flickering light bulbs. The few people sitting inside at the wrought-iron tables all leaned close to one another. Music filled the small space and people talked in whispers as if they were all there for some special clandestine meeting.

Damien waited for her in the back corner at a table for two. He already sipped on a glass of wine, which he raised to get Angelica's attention. Angelica thought this a good sign for two reasons: He drank, further confirmation that he was not a church boy, and it proved that he was more confident about the meeting than she was. She hoped this encounter would be better than last night's fiasco.

He stood as she approached the table and extended his well-manicured hand to clasp hers. "Angelica, you look fabulous, girl. I am so glad you decided to call me." His eyes freely wandered the full length of Angelica's body like they had fingers of their own. Angelica felt her eyelashes flutter as he held out the seat, helping her to sit down. She did not remember him being so handsome, but the lighting in the restaurant was dim. It was hard for anyone to be flattered by fluorescent supermarket lighting.

Damien called the waiter and ordered her a glass of wine. Angelica struggled to gain control; she wanted each action to be as she had practiced it in her mind. She needed to focus on the real reason she was here tonight. Time was short.

"Didn't you tell me you live with your grandfather? How is he?"

Angelica felt a pang of sadness and blinked back a tear. "He died a short time ago."

"I'm sorry." Damien reached across and clasped her hand again. "You must be devastated. I think trying to get out after all that is a good thing. Take your mind off of it."

Angelica smiled at the man holding her hand and realized that she was so busy trying to figure out how she was going to get the money that she had not spent much time mourning Pop-pop. For the first time, she felt abandoned, and the tears that were stored inside her sprang to her eyes. Her mascara began to run, and Angelica imagined herself with raccoon eyes. She immediately tried to wipe back her tears with the sides of her fingers, staining them black with her mascara. Damien reached into his pocket and produced a white handkerchief. He handed it to her; it was similar to the kind her grandfather always carried.

"I'm sorry, did I say something wrong?"

Angelica tried to sniff back her tears, but they kept coming. "No, I just didn't have time to realize how sad I was. I'm sorry."

"Look, we don't have to stay here if you don't feel up to it." He threw a twenty-dollar bill on the table and stood up at the same time. "Let's go. I don't live far from here. We can drink our wine in private and you won't have to worry about crying."

Angelica was relieved as he helped her to her feet. She didn't protest, letting him lead her from the small restaurant. She was sad as she thought about her grandfather, but a part of her was glad she didn't have to look for a way to get Damien from the restaurant to his apartment. Last night's experience told her that if she made a direct request it would be nothing but awkward.

Remembering the real reason she agreed to meet with Damien, she let him hold her hand as he led her the two short blocks to his apartment.

"It's not much, but it serves its purpose." Damien flicked on the light. Angelica looked around the sparsely furnished room as he opened the door. It was definitely a bachelor's pad.

"You aren't much for furniture, are you?" She wiped her eyes, still trying to clean up the mascara that was now smeared down her face.

He laughed. The living room held just a large U-shaped sofa and a big-screen television. There were no tables, knickknacks, or anything else that indicated that someone actually lived in the space. It was more sparsely furnished than a cheap motel room. Angelica could spot a small desk through the open bedroom door a few feet away.

"I thought I mentioned that I don't really live here. I'm in pharmaceutical sales and the headquarters is here. I just come here for business once or twice a month and stay for about a week. I even furnished this place from the Goodwill store. More wine?"

"Proud of that?" She nodded and accepted the wine that Damien poured for her.

"Yes, I am. I would rather conserve the money. I believe in taking the safe route. Times might not always be good." She looked around the room further and noted that there were no pictures on the wall or even any photos in the room.

The wine began to take effect and Angelica sat on the sofa, feeling herself relax some. Damien sat next to her, always clasping her hand in his own. Before long, his hand moved to her leg, and they sat together, with Angelica pretending to be interested in the ten o'clock news while she watched the hand out of the corner of her eye. She glanced at her watch and began to get anxious. The night was almost over. She leaned into Damien a little, hoping he would take the hint so the evening could progress.

"Hmmm," he said, placing his arm around her. "Are you cold?"

She shivered. "A little. "

"Well, let me warm you, then." He leaned into Angelica and brought his face close to hers. He was corny, but Angelica liked the feel of his breath on her face. She noticed his flawless skin and decided that, other than his teeth being incredibly crooked, he was not a bad-looking guy after all. If she had to give it up, she still maintained that she may as well be able to remember it positively. Damien pulled Angelica toward him, bringing his ample lips down on hers. He probed with his tongue, forcing her lips open. He simultaneously slipped his hand underneath her blouse.

"Hey! Take it easy!" Angelica was suddenly scared. She was really going through with it, and he was being rougher than she had hoped.

"What's wrong? Too fast?" Damien pulled back a little.

"No, not really. I just didn't know I was dealing with Jekyll and Hyde here. A minute ago you were so . . . different. Gentle."

"How old are you, Angelica?"

She paused. She didn't want to appear too young. "Twenty-two," she lied. He didn't flinch. Instead he reached for the wine bottle.

"You need more wine?" He added more to her glass without waiting for her answer. She didn't protest and took a big gulp. "I know you're upset about your grandfather. I won't force you. You have to forgive me for forgetting myself. It's just that you are just so attractive."

Visions of music school and New York flashed in Angelica's head. She leaned over, and this time she kissed Damien and did not stop him when he slid his hand up her thigh, reaching her crotch. He moved aside her Victoria's Secret panties, probing her with his fingers. Angelica felt herself stiffen a little, causing Damien to pause. Then, skillfully, he undressed Angelica from the waist down, and she didn't fight him. She waited as he began to undress himself, removing his shirt first. He took the time to carefully fold it and place it on the table, safely out of the way.

Angelica made no moves to stop him. She needed the deed done so she could move on.

"You have condoms, right?" she asked.

Damien smiled, but did not speak. He blinked his thick eyelashes and reached underneath the sofa. He produced a plain wooden box and flipped it open, flashing it in front of Angelica. He moved it back and forth like a waiter in a high-class restaurant showing the dessert selections. It was filled with several varieties of condoms. Angelica's mouth dropped open. He was certainly more prepared than she would have imagined. Obviously Damien was quite the player. She watched as he looked through them, appearing to choose a condom as carefully as he chose his wine. If he sniffed it, Angelica knew she would be out of there in no time.

After going through a few, he removed one from the box. Angelica put her hand on his.

"I think you should know something. I am a virgin. I need you to go slow."

"Oh, really? Then this is special, huh?" He put the condom he chose back in to the box, appearing to change his mind. "I'll use this one instead, then." He waved it in the air. "It has extra lubricant. Don't worry, I know what to do. It won't hurt very long. You know, when my wife—"

The struggle inside Angelica intensified. She could hear her grandfather preaching at her inside her head.

"Your wife? You didn't tell me you were married!" She jumped up, grabbing her clothes. A double sin would be no good. She would not be able to live with the money if she got it. A married man!

Damien looked at her, his mouth open in surprise. "Oh, did I neglect to mention that one little detail? We have a don't-ask-don't-tell agreement. She won't care."

"I am not doing this with a married man! I don't think so! So this must be your little bachelor pad where you take your women, huh?" She dressed as she spoke, slipping on her skirt and stuffing her pantyhose and underwear into her purse.

"You *are* young, aren't you? People do it all the time. It's okay, baby. And you can't go out there by yourself like this. It's not safe."

"It ain't okay with me. And it is apparently not safe in here, either. Don't call me, Damien."

"Where you going? You can't leave me like this!" Damien began to get angry. He motioned toward his penis, obviously erect beneath his underwear. "You are playing with fire, little girl!"

Angelica was out the door just in time to dodge the box of condoms flying toward her head. The box hit the floor and the contents scattered like confetti, littering the hallway outside Damien's doorway. Angelica ran the two blocks to her car like she was running a hundred-yard dash. She barely looked over her shoulder the whole way home.

Angelica was glad she'd stopped Damien. She wanted to inherit her grandfather's money, but the situation with

Damien was wrong. Every time she heard about a husband cheating on a wife, she was disgusted. Angelica could not be the other woman, not under any circumstances. Angelica knew her grandfather would not have wanted that for her. Angelica knew it wasn't what she wanted for herself, either.

14

Juan played with the reed with his tongue. He wanted to get it good and wet before he put it in his sax, to ensure that he would produce the best sounds possible. He had a ritual before he played, and he went through it in the same order every night, sometimes taking up to half an hour to get ready. First he asked the ancestors to watch over him. Then he dusted his instrument carefully before he wet his reed. James laughed at him when he caught him doing it. But there was no laughter tonight. Although he took great care not to show it, Juan was nervous tonight. He and James were waiting to meet the club's manager. It was audition night.

They listened to another gentleman playing his sax for the small crowd in the room, a Grover Washington, Jr., tune. Juan swayed as he listened; the man was good. But he still felt confident that he could blow the competition away. The brother was good, but Juan knew he was fabulous. Only one of them could be the featured amateur performer at the club at the end of the week. Juan wanted it to be him.

Juan wanted to be chosen to play here even more after he looked around the room. The place was definitely much nicer than some of the holes-in-the-wall he normally got to play in back home in the Bronx. Some of them were nothing more than a few tables set up in someone's basement. To play here would be the highlight of his trip to Baton Rouge, and it would certainly add to his résumé.

James drummed his fingers on the table. "You are so meticulous with that damn horn, but you don't want to even deal with the everyday details of the business. I don't understand you, Juan."

"It's not for you to understand. The business doesn't turn me on. The music does. I get to express my inner creativity this way. It makes me calm, like your kung fu does for you. Think of it as mind exercise."

"I see." James shrugged as he looked over Juan's shoulder. "Whatever. Anyway, you're supposed to just go up when they call your name, okay? You think you can outplay this guy? I talked you up big time to get them to hear you."

Juan smirked. "Don't be silly, man. Of course I can. You know I am the master. I thought you said it was in the bag? What happened to the cousin hookup? Not that I needed a hookup."

"Well, I want to be able to hook up other people in the future. You still gotta be good. But I think he'll hire you." Actually, James knew he would. His cousin owed him one from way back. James thought about the terrible night years ago, when he saved his four-year-old cousin from falling out of the window. James's mother was supposed to be keeping an eye on the cousin, but instead got involved in a drinking game with her latest boyfriend. James walked into his bedroom just in time to find his cousin all but dangling out of the fourth-story window, following his toy. They never told his aunt, but James carried the guilt around with him that his mother should have.

Juan and James were interrupted by someone calling Juan's name. It was time for him to play. Juan stood up confidently and strode toward the stage, sax in hand. He knew that if he looked confident, his audience would believe it, too.

He wet his lips. The room was silent in anticipation. Juan closed his eyes and visualized playing at Lincoln Center in New York, to a crowd including dignitaries from the music business. In his mind, he was the headliner, the one they all had come to see. He licked his lips again and carefully positioned his instrument. The music flowed from someplace deep inside him, and Juan could sense that everyone in the room stopped what they were doing to watch him weave his musical spell. He imagined them throwing roses at his feet.

When he finally hit the last note, the room was once again silent, and then suddenly the sparse audience began to applaud. Most were waiting for their turn to audition, but it didn't matter. They all rose to their feet and clapped for Juan and his magic sax.

He looked around the room and smiled. Mission accomplished. He knew he'd wowed them. James grinned at him from the table. Juan said "Thank you" into the mike and returned to his seat.

"Man, you are the best. Every time I hear you play, it's like the first. I keep getting reminded of why they love you so much back home, man. Ladies must always drop their panties after you play. Maybe I should take up an instrument, too."

"You stupid, man. But I love you. It has to come from the heart. You know that. I play what is in my heart." Juan thumped his chest.

"Well, from the sounds of the way you been blowing that horn, there must be a lot of shit trapped in there. But I hear you. Keep a level head and follow your heart." It was James's turn to grin. He slapped his friend a high five.

However, James couldn't help but feel that by helping Juan get what he wanted, he was betraying the trust that Big Delgado had in him. It was obvious that Juan's father was counting on him to carry on the family business and take it to the next level. James wiped his brow. He understood loyalty as much as the next man. Juan was like a brother to him, had been ever since he was little. James had eaten dinner with the Delgados many nights as a kid, not just because he felt like hanging out with his best friend, but because he was afraid to go home. James had spent too many evenings waiting on the street for his mother to get home. Sometimes she didn't come home. She went straight from her job at the post office to a nightclub or bar. She was always chasing her next meal ticket and had no concerns about whether James had dinner or not. The Delgados would look at him knowingly whenever Juan brought him home, but they wouldn't say a word. Big Delgado treated him like one of his own, often letting him spend the night, without asking any questions. Big Delgado cleaned up his scrapes, helped with his homework, and finally taught him a trade. Maybe he saved his life.

15

Deborah walked into her kitchen. She hummed to herself; things were looking up. Ché finally decided that she would help convince that girl Angelica to open her heart and her pockets to Lost Pilgrim. This was very good. They would be able to leave town before she knew it.

She put the kettle on. Hot tea was what she needed. Foster mother number three had been her favorite, and she used to say there was nothing like a good hot cup of tea to lift her spirits. Although she was already in a good mood, more good cheer couldn't hurt.

Deborah turned away from the stove toward the breakfast nook, her favorite area in the house. She loved to sit there in the mornings and look out into her yard at nature. It calmed her. Lately, with all that had been going on in the church, she needed calming more. It had gotten so hectic with the conference that it seemed like there were always a

NINA FOXX

thousand things whispering in her head. She had to keep
making a mental list of all she had to do and rehearsing it
over and over, lest she forget something. Nothing could fall
through the cracks now.

Bill sat in her space, staring into her garden. She smiled.
He seemed to be trying to find peace the way she normally
did. Deborah walked over to him from behind. She placed
her arms around his shoulders and draped herself over her
husband. She drank in his scent and smiled. She had not
been really fond of him at first. She had to force herself to
tolerate his touches, but she had come to like him and his
gentle ways a lot. He wasn't so bad. She might even be a little sad, come time to leave.

"Penny for your thoughts, honey?" She kissed him on
his ear.

Instead of leaning toward her, he moved slightly away,
but grabbed her arms to keep her from removing herself
from him.

"I'm sorry, Deb. I have a lot on my mind. Church stuff."

Deborah stiffened. Bill let her go and she straightened.
"Such as?"

"Like the board of trustees has informed me that money
is missing from the church. They can't account for where it
has gone."

The kettle screamed in the kitchen. Deborah turned
toward it, running her hand across her now-furrowed
brow. She quickly removed the kettle from the flame and
poured water on her tea bag to let it steep. If it wasn't
one thing, it was another. Here she was, thinking her

plan was finally going to go the right way, and someone was trying to stir up trouble. She'd thought she was being extra careful.

"Well, did you have them recheck their numbers? You know how easy it is to make mistakes. Half of those folks can't see straight anyway."

Bill smiled. "I told them to go back and check again, but you know they grumbled. It's almost like they can't solve any problems by themselves."

"Maybe Pilgrim needs to hire a real accountant instead of so-and-so's brother-in-law," Deborah said. She stirred her tea and wrapped the string from the hot tea bag around her spoon. A real accountant was the last thing she wanted, but Bill didn't need to know that. She pulled the tea bag back on itself, letting the excess tea dribble into the teacup.

"I guess. But if there is something wrong, I can't imagine where the money could have gone, or be going. Everything is done so carefully between the collections and the counting. The system has been working for a long time now. But you're probably right. The accounting systems are so antiquated anyway, updating couldn't possibly hurt."

Deborah didn't answer immediately. She took a sip of tea and then reached out for her husband's hand. They didn't know where the money was going because she was good. She had learned from the best, encountering criminals of all sorts during her years in the foster care system. Her eyes narrowed and she rubbed the back of his hand gently.

"It'll be okay, dear. Just wait. God will make the truth come to light." Deborah drew back her hand just as the first few drops of sweat came through to her palms. Her mind wasn't on the same truth her husband's was. Deborah was more concerned with getting what she was entitled to, the money that was rightfully hers. There was no need for her to experience poverty the way she had growing up ever again in her life. Anyone who knew and understood the truth would surely agree with her. But no one did, not yet, and Ben Chappee was dead. The time for making people understand was past. It was time for action. Deborah did not want to wait any longer.

She sipped her tea again. These people were so blind. By the time they figured it out, Deborah planned to be long gone, with revenge under her belt and her inheritance in her bank account. And then some.

16

Angelica fixed her coffee the way her grandfather liked it: one sugar, a dab of cream. She smiled to herself as she thought about the many mornings she went down to the kitchen as soon as she awoke and started the coffeepot for him. It was the morning ritual. He would always say the same thing—"One sugar, and a dot of cream?"—and Angelica would nod. It wasn't like she was going to forget the way he took it from the day before. He was gone, yet she couldn't stop herself from making coffee the same way now.

She wanted to try and get closer to her grandfather and what he was thinking when he came up with his crazy will. She had lain awake for most of the night. The rest of it was spent in that twilight place between wake and sleep where her mind played tricks on her. She kept seeing her grandfather and tried to talk to him again and again. The shadows whirled around her bed and Angelica found herself talking to them more than once.

"Why do I have to do this? I don't understand." She kept her eyes closed tightly, in the hopes the half-wake dream would stay longer. The dream in which Grandfather never answered her questions, not directly.

"You gotta read beneath the surface." It was almost as if he were talking to someone else, not her. Angelica remembered her grandfather telling her that very thing time and again while he was alive.

Why a seemingly simple task was so difficult to complete was beyond understanding. Here it was, day three, and the one thing that should be so ridiculously simple to do was making Angelica crazy. To hear men tell it, they got the drawers all the time, every time, with no problem, so what was wrong with her?

The smell of fresh coffee wafted through the house and Angelica felt warm. It was almost as if she had managed to bring her grandfather back from her dream with her, and just for a moment she felt safe again. The coffee stung her lips as she sipped it. Her grandmother used to tell her that coffee would stunt her growth, although she was the first person to ever give her any. Grandma made lattes before they were popular, putting three times the amount of milk as coffee into Angelica's cup.

She took her cup with her into the bathroom and examined her face and body thoroughly in the mirror. As far as she could tell, nothing was particularly unattractive about her; but she'd been wrong before. She thought the reason she was still a virgin was because she was saving herself for the right man. Now it seemed more like the real deal was that she was a virgin because no one wanted her in the right way. The worst part was, the only person she could count on now for reassurance was Jeanette, and the only advice she seemed to be up to offering was that Angelica should follow her heart. What the hell did that mean? Her heart was as confused as her head.

The doorbell interrupted her thoughts. Angelica was confused; she wasn't expecting anyone and did not really feel like visitors. She tried to ignore it, but the second ring told her that her caller was persistent and had no intention of leaving. The ringing changed to a knock, and she reluctantly headed toward the door, expecting a salesperson.

"Hi, Angelica. Is everything okay? My parents asked me to check on you. I decided to come over when you didn't return my call." Ché almost pushed Angelica aside to get into the room. She was short and thick, very solid. She moved Angelica's thin frame away like she was as light as a leaf. Ché's jeans rode low on her hips, and although she was well rounded, they fit as if they were made for her. The only makeup on her chestnut-brown, sharp-featured face was mascara, and her thick braids were drawn up into a knot near the top of her head.

"Ché. This is a surprise. I've been busy." Angelica could not hide her frown. What was Ché doing here?

"I understand. It must be hard. You probably have a lot to do. You have to get all your grandfather's affairs in order all by yourself." Ché glanced around Angelica's place. Having never been inside, she could not resist the temptation to examine everything she could as closely as possible.

"He took care of things for me," Angelica said.

She watched in disbelief as Ché walked around the living room and fingered whatever she wanted. It was as if her place were undergoing the white-glove test or something.

"Look, my visit is really about more than sympathy. I'm supposed to find out your intentions toward the church."

Angelica raised her eyebrows. Why was she not surprised? She blinked and was silent.

"You know, they want to know if you plan to give money to the church like your grandfather did. I heard them talking about possibly naming a nursery or something after your family in return."

"Cut right to the chase, why don't you?" Angelica shifted her weight impatiently. "I don't know what I am going to do. You folks are so bold. My grandfather always warned me about you."

Ché cocked her head to the side. "Did he, now? What did you expect? The church was his spiritual family. Always there when he needed them, right?" She fingered a small statuette, turning it over like she was looking for a price on the bottom.

"And even when he didn't, right? If he wanted to give anything to Lost Pilgrim, he would have spelled it out for me in his will."

"And what exactly did he spell out? You've been real quiet about it and we didn't hear of any large bequests in his will or anything. Surely something like that would have made the news already."

Angelica pursed her lips. Ché was fishing for information. She didn't know her too well, but it was obvious that the Davises were still not aware of the details of her grand-father's will. If they did know, she would be endlessly hounded until she gave the church something. It looked like they intended to hound her anyway.

"You can tell your folks that the church will certainly get what is coming to them. I will make sure they get whatever my grandfather wanted. Okay?"

It was Ché's turn to be silent. "All righty, then," she finally said. "On another note, how did you like the gospel conference the other night?"

"Conference?" Angelica felt the hairs on the back of her neck stand on end.

"Yeah, at the Hilton near the airport. Didn't I see you there?" Ché smiled, looking at her hands, checking for invisible dirt under her long nails. She looked up at Angelica and blinked.

"I don't think you did. I'm not into all that conference stuff."

"No, huh? I coulda sworn I saw you. In a leopard dress and these bad boots, leaving the bathroom? I tried to speak, but you were gone before I could catch you. Thought I saw you getting on the elevator, too. Or was I supposed to miss that? If you weren't at the conference, you certainly had no business going upstairs in the hotel, right?"

Angelica caught her breath. Here she was, trying to keep everything a secret, and she was spotted on the first day. By the pastor's daughter, of all people. Cloak and dagger was not for her. Her business would surely be all over the church soon, if it wasn't already.

"Don't worry, I understand. You had to find a way to let off some steam after all you are going through. I would. But who would have thought? Your Pop-pop had everyone thinking that you were such an angel. But then again, you two were always a little holier than thou, weren't you? Or are you going into a whole new line of work that we should know about?"

"Are you done, Ché? I have things to do. There's a lot on my mind." Angelica was not going to be goaded into an argument. Ché didn't matter in the scheme of things, especially if Angelica could manage to fulfill the conditions of her grandfather's will and get her inheritance. "So what are you, like, twelve years old? You have a lot of nerve."

"No, I am almost seventeen, and my age doesn't matter. I have lived a whole lot."

Angelica examined Ché's face and could see that much was probably true. Her eyes reflected experience that Angelica knew she could only imagine.

"Okay, look." Ché stepped closer to Angelica, lowering her voice to a level just above sinister. "I ain't gonna keep you. But understand me here, the church needs money. Period. Soon. And I know you can help out. Maybe you can come to the trustees meeting later this week and make a little donation in your grandfather's name?"

"And?"

"And then all our stuff will stay just between you and me? Okay?"

Angelica didn't answer. She couldn't believe what she was hearing. Tears stung her eyes. Things were getting more confusing every day and she didn't even have the money yet.

Ché opened the door herself. "Sorry I couldn't stay longer. Maybe next time you can offer me something to drink or something. Some southern hospitality." She blinked her wide-open eyes at Angelica for emphasis.

Angelica stayed rooted to her spot as Ché swept out the door, acting as if she were in a scene from *Dynasty*. Almost immediately, her doorbell rang again. She flung the door open, ready for Ché this time. What else could she possibly have to say? Her day could not get any worse.

"Are you Angelica?"

Ché was not at the door. Angelica had to look up to make eye contact. Her eyes moved upward, following the long, lanky body up to finally rest on a gorgeous face. This was no church member. Angelica was surprised by the warm smile that met her. He was the most handsome and best-dressed door-to-door salesman she'd ever seen. And he smelled good, too, enveloped in a wonderful vanilla scent.

"You have to forgive me. I should have found a way to call first. Are you Angelica? I am John Grenever. I think I've found something that belongs to you."

Angelica was still speechless but looked toward his outstretched hand. She immediately recognized her wallet; John was clutching it in his masculine, perfectly manicured hands.

"I found this in a cab two nights ago." He extended his hand. "The driver said you just got out. It didn't have a phone number in it, just your address. I know I would be in for a lot of headache if I lost my wallet."

An honest gentleman. Wow. Angelica could not believe her luck. She pushed Ché and her unexpected visit to the back of her mind. Maybe her problem would solve itself.

"Would you like to come in?" She took the wallet and smiled her warmest smile. His return smile was captivating.

He hesitated. "I am actually on my way to the airport."

"But you have to let me thank you properly. Please come in. Can I offer you a drink?"

Angelica glanced at his hand, looking for a ring. No rings, or tan lines where a ring would have been, in sight. Single.

"I do have a few minutes. I didn't know how long it would take me to get here, so I allowed extra time. Do you have a diet soda?"

"I sure do. C'mon in. Most folks would have just kept the wallet and whatever was in it." She stepped back, leading him to the sofa. "You have a seat. Where are you on your way to?"

"Oh, to Seattle. I'm from there."

"Here on business?" Angelica wondered if he had a little bachelor pad set up somewhere, like Damien.

"A little business and a little personal. I was in town visiting with my partner."

Angelica drew in her breath. She must have guessed wrong. Not everyone wore a wedding ring nowadays. "Partner? How long have you been married?"

"Oh, I am not married. My partner is Joseph Whitsmith. He's my law partner. We were visiting an old professor of his."

"Oh, so you're a lawyer?" He seemed to respond well to twenty questions.

"Yup. We have a new practice and wanted some practical advice. His professor has been in the business a long time."

"You know, let me get that diet Coke for you. I was about to change my clothes. Excuse me a minute. Make yourself at home."

Instead of going to the kitchen, Angelica made a beeline for her bedroom. Her mind was racing. Here she was, doing all this planning, and what she needed was going to fall right into her lap. She opened her lingerie drawer and quickly searched for the new teddy she'd bought from Victoria's Secret. She threw her clothes on the bed and pulled it on. Then she stood back and admired herself in the mirror. If this didn't get him, nothing would.

Angelica grabbed a bathrobe, drawing it loosely around her. She took a bottle of perfume from her dresser and spritzed herself behind her ears. She sniffed; she smelled good enough to eat.

She smoothed her robe, opening the bedroom door. She wanted to appear calm, as if what was happening were normal.

John was standing outside the door with a can of diet Coke in his hand.

He raised it as he spoke. "I hope you don't mind. I helped myself."

"No, no problem. That's good, really." Angelica tried to find her sexiest voice, and John glanced down, almost dropping his Coke.

"Sorry."

"No apology necessary, you caught it. Now, where were we?"

John opened his mouth, but before he could answer, his cell phone rang. Angelica smiled as the phone chimed "The Yellow Rose of Texas." This was a sign! The same song the doorbell played. He strode back into the living room, with Angelica close behind. She listened to him talk in short, staccato sentences. He was nervous and she liked that she was having that effect on him. Wetness began to form between her legs. She couldn't tell if she was getting excited because he was attractive or because she might get her inheritance after all.

Angelica's guest sat on the couch, and she stood behind him, waiting for him to get off the phone.

"I'm sorry, Angelica. You were saying?"

"I wasn't. You helped yourself to the diet Coke I offered, and I freshened up. Would you like anything else?"

"No, thanks. I really have to be going." He stood up, shifting his weight from foot to foot.

"So soon? I thought we could talk more. I really appreciate what you have done. You saved me a lot of trouble. To tell the truth, I didn't even realize I had left my wallet in that cab." She came around the couch, now standing between John and the door. She wanted him to be able to take in the full view. His nervousness became even more obvious as he made an effort to look everywhere in the room but at Angelica.

"Well, miss, you should be more careful. Not everyone would have returned the wallet. Or worse yet, they could use your information to harm you. All your personal information is in there."

"I know. I was a little frazzled and in a hurry when I left it in the cab." Angelica moved to make sure that John had no choice but to look at her. She let her robe fall strategically open, showing almost all of her shapely thighs. Beads of sweat were starting to form on his brow, making Angelica feel more confident.

His phone shrilly rang out again, and this time he answered without excusing himself. Angelica could tell by the way he pursed his lips that he was annoyed. She was standing so close to him that she couldn't help listening.

His voice was stern. "I told you that that color was all wrong for the study. I'm going to be home soon anyway." He flipped his phone closed.

Angelica was confused. He said he wasn't married, but he seemed to be having a quarrel with someone very close.

"My partner." He pursed his lips. "I am sorry. And might I say that is damn nice lingerie."

"You have a study in your law practice? You must have big offices." She moved a little, subtly suggesting that she was modeling her outfit for him.

"I wasn't talking to my law partner, but my life partner. We've been together for several years. We just bought a house and he's doing some decorating. He always waits until I'm gone to make major decisions."

Angelica gulped. "Life partner?"

"Yes, Angelica. I am gay. Oh, girl, I hope you didn't think . . .?"

"No, no. I'm sorry to look surprised." She drew her robe back around her body, once again concealing her new underwear. Her face burned with embarrassment.

"Thank you for bringing my wallet. Don't you have to go?"

"Angelica, it's not personal. You really are a beautiful girl. But you should be more careful about whom you let into your apartment while you're dressed like that. I could have been a psycho or something. I hope I didn't lead you on. It really is nice lingerie, though."

Angelica felt annoyed and dejected. It hadn't been easy up to now, so she didn't know why she felt it would suddenly turn that way. She also knew she didn't need to be lectured, and she felt her frustration quickly turning to anger. And now she had blackmail hanging over her head, too.

"Well, thanks for that wisdom," she snapped. "You can go now. I *do* appreciate what you did. You can take the Coke with you." She motioned toward the door.

John looked as if Angelica had slapped him, but she didn't care. She walked toward the door to give him a further hint, and he followed. She stood aside so that he could leave, without saying good-bye. Angelica slammed the door behind him so hard she surprised herself.

No sooner had she turned around than Angelica felt herself begin to lose control. What a way to begin the morning! Her chest began to heave and she leaned back against the door. She had never hyperventilated before, but she wondered if this was what it felt like. Her ears felt hot and the room swayed back and forth. Not wanting to fall, she sat on the floor, legs bent. She put her head between her legs like she had seen done on television. This whole ordeal was turning into a big mess.

She pressed her eyes closed until she saw white spots and counted to ten. Angelica was not wearing much, but she suddenly felt hot. It took her ten minutes to eventually get hold of herself. She moved to the sofa and called Jeanette.

Jeanette sounded groggy, as if she'd been asleep, but Angelica knew Jeanette would listen to her. She always did. Tears started to flow down her cheeks and she choked back sobs as the words tumbled out of her mouth. Having to earn her inheritance was one thing, but this problem with Ché was way too much for her to handle alone.

Jeanette listened quietly, waiting for a break in Angelica's onslaught of words and emotion.

"Did you think they weren't going to ask you for money? They ask everyone else's family that dies. What made you think you would be different?"

"This *is* different. I think that girl threatened me. You should have heard what she said." Her voice was full of disbelief.

"She is so asinine. You know you can step on that hen if you wanted to. You want me to do it?"

Angelica sniffed and laughed. Jeanette was making her feel better already.

"You just ignore her," Jeanette continued. "You know, I really thought the mother was the crazy one. It might still be. I can't see Ché doing something like this on her own. You know what they say about them, don't you?"

Angelica pursed her lips. "What? That they're predatory? You know I try not to listen to all that church gossip stuff."

"No, girl. You should have listened to this. I halfway believe it, too, because it keeps coming up. The way I hear it, crazy runs in their family."

"I thought you had some real news. Folks are just jealous because Deborah is the pastor's wife."

"Nu-uh. From what I hear, Miss Deborah's mother killed herself. Was crazy as a bedbug. She jumped out of a hospital window, right after Deborah was born. The baby was sooo ugly, she couldn't take it." Jeanette laughed. "Why do you think we can't open windows in public buildings anymore?"

"Okay, see? You ain't right." Angelica chuckled. "That's just mean."

"Seriously, she did kill herself. I didn't get the whole story. I'm surprised your grandfather didn't tell you about it. My father says that's what he and the pastor fell out over. This all happened back in Baltimore, and then Deborah and Ché show up here all these years later. Did you even know that Deborah was from the same place your grandfather was?"

The plot was thickening. Pop-pop was a lot more secretive than Angelica had known. He'd never mentioned this to her; in fact, when she tried to talk about how he'd parted ways with the pastor, he told her to stay out of grown folks' business. He knew that hurt her. It couldn't matter now, though.

"No wonder Ché had that wild look in her eyes. But that's all water under the bridge now, huh?"

"I guess it is. I gotta go. Time to make the donuts!"

They hung up.

Water under the bridge. Angelica wondered. She wasn't too sure. For a minute, she wondered if her grandfather's past was going to come back to haunt her.

17

Juan was ecstatic. Nothing could go wrong today, or during the rest of the time he would be in Baton Rouge. Not even the phone call from his father could put a damper on that. Big Delgado had called right in the middle of Juan's deliveries, to check on what he and James were doing. Juan had made the mistake of telling him about his audition, and his father had yelled at him for fifteen minutes about wasting his time. Big Delgado was insensitive and inflexible, refusing to see things any other way but his own. Compromise was not even a possibility. Juan was so flustered after the call, he actually had to refer to James's maps three times.

After his stellar audition, Juan was chosen to be the featured amateur performer in the club at the end of the week, just like he knew he would be. What did his father think now? Would he still dismiss Juan's musical talents as a waste of time? When Juan got home, he would find a way to sit down with his father and make him understand how he felt. He had to find a way to do what he loved. It didn't matter if he might not ever get real famous doing it.

He had his gig all planned out in his head. He would start with something mellow and warm up the crowd. He would pick up the intensity gradually during the fifteen minutes he was given, work the crowd up into a frenzy. He thought about it so much that it was almost impossible to keep his mind on the business at hand, that of picking up and delivering robes.

He headed toward the Church of the Lost Pilgrim. Today he was supposed to pick up robes from the choir at the church. Their choir was rehearsing there, away from the conference hotel. This choir was one of the largest single groups performing, and supposedly among the best. They wanted to keep their musical numbers a secret until the last minute, and that didn't make it any easier for Juan.

It was hard to concentrate on the road as he visualized himself playing to the crowd at the end of the week. Juan had to keep checking the map. Not that he could miss the church. Off to the right, he could see the massive building coming into view. Impressive. It stood off to the side of the road, almost alone. The huge church building was obviously very new or very well kept. Juan chuckled to himself. They must have had one hell of a church building fund. As he got closer, Juan could see that it actually spread out into several wings. It even had its own bus stop. The ultramodern building resembled an office complex more than a church.

Juan drove his truck around the huge parking lot. It was so big, he wondered if there were shuttle buses that went from the outer lots of the church to the front door before services. Back home, churches were big, but nothing like this. There was just no space. The closest thing to this was the Allen A.M.E. Church out in Queens. Juan recalled that the Allen Church had everything, including nursing home facilities.

Although it wasn't Sunday, the lot appeared to be pretty full. Juan ended up parking across from the church in a strip mall. Although this did not appear to be the best part of town, it looked safe. Juan did not doubt that the strip mall probably got a lot of business from the church anyway. Not that there was that much there: A gas station and convenience store. A corner newsstand, almost like the kind back home. A Vietnamese restaurant. And a liquor store.

Juan smiled. Now, that was amusing. People could go to church, and afterward they could come outside, cross the street, and grab something to drink. No doubt some did. This was an interesting neighborhood. Liquor stores and churches, all in there together. Juan guessed he wouldn't have to look too hard to find the inevitable funeral home, either.

Juan crossed the street, still rehearsing his performance in his head, barely paying attention to where he was walking. Good thing there was no real traffic, or he would have been crushed for sure.

No one spoke to Juan as he walked into the massive narthex. The church was bustling with activity. Everyone seemed to be in a hurry.

Juan could hear the choir singing before he saw them. They were indisputably good, and he already knew they were large by the sheer amount of robes that he was asked to pick up and deliver almost daily. They were singing a song Juan recognized from the radio. It was by one of those newfangled gospel groups that had rappers in their midst. By the sounds of things, Juan could tell a few of the folks were probably not far from dancing.

"Can I help you?" a young man greeted Juan. His pants were way too far down and appeared to be one step away from dropping to his ankles. Juan had missed him originally; the young man was standing in the hallway with a phone attached to his ear. He stood with his back to the door, probably talking to a girl, but he'd paused in his conversation.

"Yeah, man. I'm here to pick up the robes to be cleaned for tomorrow. I'm from the Delgado Brothers?"

The young man reached up and extracted a pencil, previously propped behind his ear, half held in place by his small Afro. He used it to point down the hall. Then he continued his phone conversation, without saying anything else to Juan.

Juan headed in the direction he'd pointed. The church looked even bigger from the inside. Juan made his way past several rooms, all of them containing people rehearsing, talking, or just hanging out. There were kids everywhere. He was amazed; back home it seemed to be hard to get kids to go anywhere near a church on the weekends, much less during the week. But at least they weren't hanging out on the corners or across the street at the liquor store.

Juan reached the end of the hall. A sign above the double door indicated that he had found the choir room. He pushed the doors open and found what he was looking for. The robes were placed in a large, used-to-be-white rolling bin. A small miracle. Up to this point, he dreaded the several trips he thought he would surely have to make back and forth to where the van was parked. A bin would make the job much easier. It must have been James's idea. He had a way of thinking of everything, just like Pops said he did.

Juan grabbed the bin and began to push it, the wheels squeaking in protest. He started back down the long hallway, continuing to look around. He passed a door he had not noticed before. THE PASTORAL OFFICES, according to the sign. Very formal.

"Young man?" Someone from inside called to him. Juan stopped, taking a step back to look inside the slightly open door. The voice came from behind a large mahogany desk, the largest Juan had ever seen. No fancy desks like that at the Delgado Brothers. It reminded Juan of his grandmother's dining room table, the one they never sat at except for very special occasions.

"Yes?"

"You from the cleaners?"

"Yes. I am Juan Delgado." He waited.

"Well, why didn't you say so? I'm Bill Davis, the pastor here. I didn't know they were sending the big boss!" The pastor stepped around his desk, striding toward Juan with his hand outstretched.

Juan took it and the man began to pump his arm up and down. He returned the smile.

"No, sir. The big boss would be my father. Glad we could be of service."

"I'm glad that we could help a minority-owned business get the contract. An old-fashioned family-owned business, at that. It's very nice to meet you. Hopefully we will see you in church on Sunday?"

Juan fidgeted. "Well, we're going to have to work 'round the clock to make sure everyone has a clean robe. But thanks for the invitation."

"You are always welcome. We like visitors here at Lost Pilgrim. Let me know if there's anything you need, son, okay?"

"Like the bathroom? Nature's calling." Juan grinned as the pastor pointed his way. "Nice meeting you."

Juan left the bin outside the bathroom door and stepped inside. From the stall, he could hear female voices loud and clear. For a moment he thought he was in some sort of co-ed bathroom, but then he noticed a vent in the wall next to him. The voices came through from another room, obviously connected to the bathroom via this vent. Juan stood with his feet glued in place. He couldn't help but listen.

"Ma, I ain't so sure this is a good idea. What if she doesn't go for it?"

"Ché, you scared that girl so good, she will have to give money to the church. Then all our troubles will be over."

"Why should she, Ma? She hardly comes. And when she does, she doesn't look happy and she leaves right after. I can't believe you got me mixed up in your mess anyway."

"My mess is your mess. And you know as well as I do that we deserve it. If Angelica does what you say, then we can get out of here. And what do you mean my mess? You started this thing."

Juan stepped out of the stall. He didn't bother to wash his hands. He didn't want to hear any more of what those women were talking about, and he set his mind on getting out of the church as fast as he could. He hurried down the hall, remembering why he was reluctant to attend church and even more reluctant to get involved in one. Religion was too private an affair, and it certainly didn't have anything to do with all the gossip and mess that seemed to go on. Whatever those women were talking about surely had no relation whatsoever to the personal salvation their pastor surely preached about on Sundays, and it certainly had nothing to do with dry cleaning.

Juan left the church building and pushed the cart across the street toward the truck. He passed behind the newsstand, looking at the ground. He didn't know what those women were talking about, but he knew he didn't want to meet up with them.

A voice coming from the newsstand caught his ear and

Juan looked up. He was immediately in awe. Standing across from him was the most beautiful creature he had ever seen. He stopped behind his truck, almost paralyzed. He could not believe his eyes. The woman had her head down and seemed to be fumbling for money. She moved lyrically, almost in slow motion. Juan was entranced. Music played in his head again, but this time he was not rehearsing. He watched as she looked in her bag, picked up a paper, and conversed with the man who operated the newsstand. They talked, she laughed and tossed her head back slightly. Juan could tell she was very comfortable with the man. She was probably from around here and had known that man all her life. It appeared to be such an easy conversation. Relaxed.

She finished her business and walked away, newspapers under her arm. Juan stared after her. He couldn't help but feel like he'd met her somewhere before, another life, maybe. She disappeared around the corner, and Juan continued to stare at the place where she had been. He blinked and exhaled. He should have talked to her. Why couldn't he move? A car passed, the robes he placed in the bin fluttered in the wind. Juan opened the doors to the back of the truck. He had met some fine women before, but none who affected him like the one he just saw. It was as if her beauty came from somewhere within, and Juan could not shake the feeling of déjà vu. He closed the doors to the truck and he knew he and that woman would meet again. Soon. He hoped.

He drove away from the church slowly. His mind was no

longer on music. His thoughts floated between the women he heard in the bathroom and the one he saw at the newsstand. He imagined the women he overheard to be as unattractive as their conversation, in direct contrast to the woman he had just seen. He drove in the direction she had walked, but did not catch a glimpse of her again.

18

Deborah paused in her conversation with Ché. A young woman from the choir walked into the restroom.

"Hello, Sister Davis. Ché." They both nodded at her without answering as they waited for her to do her business and leave. Ché looked at her fingers as the woman washed her hands. Deborah tapped her foot. The atmosphere was uncomfortable enough that their visitor left quickly.

The door closed slowly behind her, too slowly for Deborah. Her robes rustled as she took a step closer to her daughter, as if someone might be listening in the otherwise empty bathroom.

"You don't understand. There are things you don't know." She hissed at Ché, a snakelike quality in her voice.

Ché rolled her eyes. She was getting tired of her mother's schemes. This was their third church in eight years, at least that she could remember, and it was the same story every time. This was the third time for her mother as a pastor's wife. Ché had hoped that she would get it right this time. She narrowed her saucerlike eyes at her mother.

"There must be. Your formula was working so well. Why do you have to add blackmail to it? You usually don't bother anyone, and I usually get to act like I don't know what's going on, Ma. I am not a baby anymore. I know the game. Don't forget, I was the one who saw the personal ad in the first place. I was the brains in this thing."

"This is my deal." Deborah thumped her chest. "You just gotta come along a little while longer, that's all. Besides, we are entitled to that money. And you owe me, remember? My life changed when you were born. Did you forget that? And yes, you were the one that saw the ad, but you saw it because I wanted you to."

Ché took a step back. She looked at her mother's face, seeing desperation in her eyes that she had not noticed before.

"What do you mean?" She leaned back on the sink, her arms crossed.

"I mean, I needed you to buy in to this move. I had to get closer to Ben Chappee. I thought he would know me when he saw me." Deborah opened her black compact and reapplied her foundation.

Ché frowned. That was the third time she'd done that since they came into the bathroom. Deborah was losing it. This whole thing with scheming to get to know Angelica to get her to donate money that she knew her mother was going to take was bizarre, too bizarre even for Deborah. And she was tired of hearing about the morbid circumstances of her birth. It was done. Life goes on, whether Deborah wanted it to or not.

"Ma, what are you talking about? You didn't have to have me, you know. I know the story, you loved each other, blah, blah, blah."

"Don't be fresh. I will not tolerate it." Deborah stood up. She clenched and unclenched her fists, her face darkening. Ché took a step back. "They would have adopted me. He would have been my adopted brother. If you had not happened, no one ever would have known about he and I. And I had to have you, I had no money to pay for an abortion. You're here now, you just need to go along with what I want. Until you're an adult, you just do what I say."

Deborah's words stung. Ché swallowed the anger and hurt she felt rising in her throat. Sometimes she hated her mother, but she was scared of her, too. Ché had heard all of this before, but none of that could be changed now. She gulped. "I don't understand. Usually you just leave if people think something is happening. Does someone know that something is going on? Are they pointing fingers at you? We could just leave. We've done it before."

"We could, but we're not going to, not this time. This thing is different. There are things here that started way before you were born. You just don't let your part get out of hand, okay? Trust me, you will understand eventually, I promise. I got to get back to the rehearsal." Deborah turned to the mirror and checked her makeup again.

"It's under control." Ché wanted to calm her mother, make it all right for her. "I do believe Miss Thing is going to come around." She winked. She wanted her mother to feel calm, but she was beginning to worry. Deborah was usually much calmer than this.

"Well, it better be. Time is getting short," Deborah snapped. She opened the door to the restroom and stepped back so Ché could walk through it in front of her. Devoid of the privacy the restroom offered them, they were both silent. Deborah looked down the hallway nervously. The door to her husband's office was open, as always. Other than that, the only person in the hallway was a delivery-man, wheeling a cart down at the other end.

19

The fourth night. Angelica sat deep in thought while the television blared in the background watching her. She needed to take drastic measures to accomplish her task. Time was running out and she was no closer to getting her inheritance. She was caught in the middle of so much. If she did what her grandfather asked in the will, she would have enough money to do whatever she wanted, maybe for the rest of her life.

She sighed, her heart heavy. She would eventually lose her virginity anyway. On the other hand, if she went ahead and did what her grandfather asked in the will, then she would be expected to give heaven knows what sum of money to the church. They would hound her to death for sure. And would it stop there? Ché had sounded serious. Sure, they might name a day-care center or nursing home after her grandfather, but how could she be sure Ché wouldn't be back for more money later?

Angelica just could not see a win-win situation for anybody.

Looking for Love by Carl Webber lay on the coffee table. Angelica had fallen asleep earlier reading it; it was about a phone. Why not hire someone for the job? A love line would take too long; she wasn't looking for love anyway, just sex. The television and classifieds were full of ads for male gigolos and such—that might be the best route. That way there would be no mistaking the purpose, no chance of the person hanging around, and certainly no procrastinating. She thought about dropping by the newsstand and dressed to go out. The back of the *New Voice* newspaper was always littered with pages and pages of solutions. She tied the laces on her sneakers and shook her head. She couldn't believe that this was what her Pop-pop really intended. Angelica could almost see him, in her head, making jokes about this one. She wondered if he ever thought she would resort to this.

The newsstand was just around the corner. Angelica was pensive as she walked the short distance. Her footsteps were heavy, and she tried hard to understand what made Ché think her grandfather would give more in his will than he gave in life to the Church of the Lost Pilgrim. Although he disagreed with a lot that went on there, he did feel that it was necessary to give to the church. It was his way of giving back to his community. He even headed the building fund drive last year. His name was engraved in the cornerstone of the building. Still, if he had wanted the church to benefit from his death, he would have made provisions in his will, but he didn't.

The newsstand was small and old-fashioned. The small radio there had been tuned to a talk radio station for as long as Angelica could remember. The man behind the counter used to scare Angelica when she was smaller. One of her earliest memories was of passing the newsstand, the man in the booth smiling his toothless grin and calling out to all the passersby. He would talk back to the radio, and the neighborhood kids would make fun of him and his snaggletoothed grimace.

"Hey, Angelica. How you? Sorry to hear about your loss."

"Thanks, Mr. Williams. I'm fine. You got a *New Voice* in there?"

She opened her purse, not wanting to make eye contact. He handed her the paper.

"That un's free. Don't you want to read a real paper? That's trash. Newfangled trash."

Angelica smiled. She felt almost obligated to buy something else. "Sure I do. How 'bout the *News?* Let me have one of those, too."

Angelica fished in her purse again for some change. She really didn't want to read the *News,* but Ben needed to make a living and the *New Voice* was free. She handed him his money and glanced across the street at the parking lot of the church. It was packed. The gospel convention was larger than she had thought it would be. All the church parking lots and hotels in the downtown area were full, just like the one at Lost Pilgrim. She turned her back to the church and headed toward home, hoping the solution to her problems was now safely tucked under her arm.

Angelica barely got through her door before she dropped the *News* onto the floor. She flopped down on her sofa, planning to read the *New Voice* from the back. That was where the information she needed was. Those ads seemed to always start after the personals.

Angelica nervously tapped her foot as she turned the pages. Most of the ads seemed to be directed at men. If she were a man, she would have no problem; there was plenty of information on how to get a live woman to come to your hotel room or home. There were plenty of ads for strip clubs, too. Her stomach churned.

There had to be male ads in here somewhere. There seemed to be plenty when you didn't want them. What type of person would do this kind of work? How much was it going to cost her? She hoped it was safe. She would be sure to make him wear double condoms. A girl couldn't be too safe in this day and age.

Angelica flipped through the newspaper for about ten minutes. She passed personal ads, ads for sex toys, ads for women seeking women and men seeking men. There were even adds for couples seeking a third and all other sorts of strange things. But she couldn't seem to find what she needed.

Wait, what was this? *Sexy, clean men for discriminating ladies. Call 1-888-AAA-LOVE.* She read the fine print and chuckled to herself. *Always discreet and professional.* Hmmm. The man in the ad looked reasonably attractive and clean, with long hair. The picture was small, but it looked okay. Angelica smiled. This was it. He would definitely do. He would have to. Please let this work, she thought.

She snatched the phone off the hook. Angelica dialed and waited. Finally, it was answered on the fifth ring. The reality of the situation hit her. She was calling a male prostitute. A paid gigolo. This was worse than an XXX movie.

"Um, is this the hotline? The place where . . ." She could feel the phone becoming slippery in her hand.

"We provide qualified male escorts for discriminating ladies of taste. I can hear the nervousness in your voice. There is no need to be anxious. Our gentlemen are professional and they take pride in what they do. Do you have a racial preference?" The woman on the phone spoke matter-of-factly, as if nothing were strange or out of place.

Angelica cleared her throat. "No, he just needs to be tall."

"Tall. Okay. Would that be over or under six feet? We can try to get you exactly what you need."

Angelica licked her lips. Her palms were sweating and her foot was bopping up and down a mile a minute. This was like ordering takeout. "How about right around six feet?"

"That we can do. Do you have other requirements? Will you be attending a function?"

"Well, is there a difference in the fees?" Angelica's voice wavered.

"This is your first time doing this, isn't it? Let me assure you that there is no need to be nervous. Everything we do here is strictly confidential. Our rates start at five hundred for an hour and go up from there, depending on the occasion and services you choose. What did you have in mind?"

"I was thinking about an intimate evening at home. Maybe dinner."

"Many of our clients ask for that. That is not hard to accommodate, especially if a tuxedo is not required. If he is meeting you locally, our basic hourly rate is where we would start. The fee is paid directly to the escort at the end of the night. We can accept credit cards, but not checks if you are a new client."

Angelica gulped.

"You can think about it and call back if you like."

She had not anticipated the cost being so high. It had better be worth it. She would really have to dig into her savings. "No, that's fine. Is anyone available for tonight?"

She took a deep breath, gave the woman on the phone her address, and chose eight o'clock as the meeting time. She needed time to get ready. She looked around the living room and began to pick up the cups and magazines she'd left laying around the past few days. Stress was starting to get to her and it was beginning to show around the house. She had not been in her grandfather's part of the house since he had died.

She got the room as straight as she could, managing to remove the thin layer of dust from obvious places. She walked into her bedroom, intending to shower and get dressed. She decided her jeans and her sweater were fine. She was paying, so he had better like what he got.

20

Juan backed his truck onto the loading dock at the plant. He bumped into the wall, and the gate on the truck flew open. He jumped down, kicking papers away as he walked around the back. James was waiting for him.

"Man, you got rocks in your head or what? The whole building moved when you backed in here." James scratched his head. "And you talk about my driving. Yours ain't much better."

"Lay off me, man. Mission accomplished, okay? The robes are in the truck, and they are here, on time, like they are supposed to be!"

James looked down at his clipboard and marked it with his pencil. "Well, at least one thing is good today. Why do you have that silly grin across your face?"

"Things are great, man. I just had a vision—"

"Oh, here we go with that stuff again. You need to stay

163

away from that wacky weed." James turned back toward the plant. Juan followed.

"You know I don't do nothing like that, man. Seriously, I just saw the most beautiful woman I have ever seen in my life. It was magic, like I met her before."

"Really?" James paused and let his clipboard drop to his side. "Well, well. Where? Did you talk to her? Did you get the digits? Did you work some of your magic on her?" He grinned, letting Juan catch up to him. He slapped his friend on the back.

"That's the funny thing. I saw her outside the church after my delivery at Lost Pilgrim. But I couldn't move, couldn't say a word. I was paralyzed. I just watched her. She didn't even see me. I can't believe it. That type of thing has never happened to me before."

"Man, I don't know why you are wasting your time. You ain't going to be here very long anyway. You need to make some moves, take action when you can."

"I know all that. But I was powerless. Besides, you know, if it was meant to be . . . Besides, I got other things on my mind anyway. Like my performance."

"Yeah, and dry cleaning." James laughed, motioning with his clipboard.

"That, too." Juan smiled for the first time in hours. James never let up. Although Juan did not talk to the girl, he felt better than he had since he'd arrived in Baton Rouge. Maybe being here wasn't so bad. He would get to play his music and he'd seen the most beautiful girl in the world. He felt better than he had in a long time.

The two friends walked back into the building, rolling the cart that Juan had picked up with them. It was well past quitting time. His legs were heavy and his brows had been knit so long from concentrating that even they were tired. He rubbed at them with his thumb in an attempt to relieve the tension that he just realized he was feeling. He stretched his back.

"James," he said. "Some good music in a nice atmosphere would do me real good right about now."

"I'm with you. I been standing around here all day in this sweatbox. I need some kind of escape, too. I know just the place. Let's head over to my cousin's."

They pushed the cart into its spot. "I just want to sit and listen. And be mellow."

"I'm with you, Jefe." He turned to go back to the main office. "By the way, your father called today."

Juan sucked in his breath. He had been waiting for James to make some business-related comments for what seemed like hours. After last time, he could tell his friend had more to say to him.

"And he said to make sure—"

"Make sure what? If he didn't think we could handle it, why did he send us? Is he going to check up on us every minute?" Juan walked through the office door, slamming it back against the wall. He turned around to face James, who had followed him. "Or is he just going to have you check up on me?" His eyes narrowed.

James stood silent. The air in the room felt suddenly heavy to him, but charged with electricity. There was only so much of Juan and his selfishness that he could take.

"You don't get it, do you? You have everything given to you, and it's still not enough. I have been very quiet, but you are bordering on disrespect. Is what he is asking really all that difficult?" He crossed his arms and looked at Juan. He could see that his response had surprised him.

"I told you I—"

"Can we make it not about you for a change? Why do you have to see the two things—what you want, music; and what he wants, some responsibility on your part—as mutually exclusive? They don't have to be, you just want them that way. Why can't you do both until you figure out the next step? Why do you find it necessary to disrespect you father and throw away what he is trying to give you?"

"What would you know about it?" He growled at James. "I really don't see this as your business. We all know there ain't nobody leaving you a thing. That is the only reason you are even concerned for me."

James's heart stung. He could not believe what he was hearing. "Okay, we obviously need to go and get a drink, because you have lost every bit of your mind. What I see is that this ain't about me. I see your selfishness blinding the hell out of you and that you have no regard for the feelings of the man who busted his behind to take care of you, and for that matter me, too. We need to talk about this some other time." He picked up some papers and slammed them down on the desk.

Juan was sorry for his words the minute they'd left his mouth. "I'm sorry, man. You're right. I gotta think this all through. I am going to sit down and talk to Papi as soon as we get back. Maybe we can work it out where I am a consultant to the business after a while or something."

"It's about time you started to think about things. No one wants to listen to you if you are so angry all the time. You ain't getting any younger. I'm helping you out because I love you. Your family just wants to make sure that you can take care of yourself after they are gone. You're like family to me. And unlike you, I truly believe that people get what they deserve."

Juan ran his fingers through his hair. "And I deserve a drink right now." He paused, waiting for a reaction from James.

James looked up at him. He knew better than to think his friend had understood his meaning so quickly. There were some things people had to learn for themselves. He didn't want to escalate the issue, not now. "You are absolutely right. I think I deserve one, too." He patted his pockets to check for his wallet and then headed for the door.

21

Deborah sat in her reading chair, but it was hard to concentrate. Usually the warmth of the chair would help her read comfortably, but lately it just lulled her deeper into the shadows of her mind. Her life was confusing and it was becoming more and more difficult to concentrate. The plan she had in the beginning was getting lost. She sat and stared at her page, finally realizing she had not read a word on it. Most of the book was a blur.

Thoughts of her husband Bill and how she came to know him haunted her. She found herself dwelling on how she had willingly married a man so much older than she was. She needed to at the time; it was the only way she could get close to Ben Chappee, who had been Bill's best friend. How was she to know that they would argue and stop speaking? She had not counted on that. Or on Ben dying before she could get them to mend their friendship.

Bill walked past and called her name softly.

She looked down at the clock on the table next to her. He was home much earlier than she had thought he would be.

"Bill. I thought you would be at the meeting a few more hours." She smiled weakly. "How'd it go?"

"You know. Same stuff. It went. They're still talking about the church finances." He paused, as if waiting for an answer or at least some acknowledgment of what he'd said. Instead, Deborah appeared to have slipped back into her trance.

"Deb? You okay? You have been very weird lately. I know it has been difficult, but all this will pass."

Deborah could not keep herself from thinking about Angelica Chappee and her grandfather. Over the past few months, she'd watched them secretly. She yearned to know more about the Chappee family. The argument between Chappee and Bill that she'd thought would only last a few weeks had gone on for two years.

"I'm fine." She smiled. "How well did you know Ben Chappee? Were you friends?"

Bill sighed. His wife was obviously somewhere else. The first few months had been blissful, but how long had he expected that to last? He'd found her on the Internet, after all. They didn't really know each other. She'd answered his personal ad. An answer to his dreams. She was young, and when they finally met, she was wonderful. Deborah was everything a pastor could want in a wife. But she had become withdrawn lately. It was obvious something was bothering her, something serious that she had yet to share with him. He hated to think that Ben had been right about her after all.

"I knew him for years. I wouldn't say we were friends in recent years. Why?"

"No reason." Deborah looked at her book.

"Deb, are you happy with me? I wish you would talk to me about what is going on." He couldn't put his finger on it, but whatever it was had to do with Ben Chappee. She'd seemed preoccupied with him and his family from the very start. Even more interesting was the fact that Ben didn't like her from the very beginning. If Bill didn't know better, he would think that Ben was right on target when he said her turning up in Baton Rouge was more than a co-incidence, especially with her link to their hometown. They'd argued about it before they ever got to talk about it. Ben had wanted Bill to investigate Deborah's back-ground more and confront her. He couldn't do it. He knew she would be the perfect wife. It was certainly too late to talk about it now.

Deborah looked at her husband, almost feeling a pang of tenderness. He didn't understand; he couldn't. This was about much more than just the two of them. It was about re-venge, getting what she was entitled to. But he didn't need to know all that. There was no way she could tell him all of the details. Not even Ché knew everything. She had searched for years and could not believe it when an oppor-tunity to get closer to Ben presented itself. It was almost too easy. Ché thought they were just going to skim a little money off the top and then move on to the next place. Deb-orah could never come to tell her the truth.

"Do you love me, Deb? Don't you trust me?" Bill looked

at his wife. He knew there was that little part of her she was not sharing.

"Of course I do, Bill. I'll be fine." Deborah rolled her eyes. She was beginning to lose her patience. The voice in her head that had become all too familiar was screaming at her. Things were getting muddled enough without him asking questions. He needed to sit tight a little while longer. Deborah refused to be sidetracked. The less he knew, the better. "I just have been a little under the weather lately. Not able to concentrate, you know, a thousand things going on at once. I'm sure I'll be fine."

Bill backed off. He wanted to allow his wife her privacy. Her life had been hard for her, he knew that much. She had only told him a little about the years she'd spent in foster care, but he knew it was probably rougher than she was letting on. It had to be painful for her to talk about. The little she told him made him just want to take care of her. All those years of uncertainty and moving around had to have taken their toll on her.

Ché nervously peeked into her mother's open bedroom door. She knew she had only a few minutes at best; whenever her mother and the pastor did not invite guests past the front room where they now sat, the guests would only stay a little while.

She held on to the little key in her hand so hard that the hole at the top was making indentations in her fingers. The red velvet box was sitting on the table where it always was, and Ché could only hope the key would work. The one she had seen her mother use to open the box looked like a luggage key, but it had never dawned on her before to try to use an actual luggage key to open the lock. Most luggage keys were interchangeable, so Ché felt she had a chance.

The thought of looking in the box never crossed her mind before, but her mother was getting stranger and stranger and Ché needed to know more. She sat for hours, reading the book that was in that box or holding on to what looked like old letters. And Ché had caught her talking to herself more than once lately.

Ché tiptoed across the floor, even though the tan Berber carpet would more than cushion her footsteps. She strained her ears, making sure the voices from the living room kept up their chatter and stayed where they were.

The red box was the only thing on the table other than a television remote. It was velvet and quilted on the top. The small lock looked as if it were added as an afterthought. When she was a little girl, Ché remembered being scolded once about touching the box. It disappeared for a while and she never thought about it again. It resurfaced when they moved to Baton Rouge, this time with the small lock on the top.

The key fit right into the lock and turned easily, snapping the box open with the first try. Ché looked over her shoulder and flipped up the padded top. The box was deep. She pushed aside some small items and removed the book she was looking for. It was old-fashioned, with thick papers. She flipped through it carefully. A page with a dark ink blot caught her eye. It had holes in it as if someone had stabbed at the page with a pen time and time again.

January 15, 1967

I know he loves me. I don't care that he is older and can't talk to me during the day. Ma'dear went to the church picnic but said I was sick so I didn't have to go. No one wants me there anyway. I don't know why folks here are so different than they are down home, but I don't fit in.

I knew B. would come over if I invited him. He practically ran over as soon as the car drove off. We were together, right in my bed, and his strong arms held me. I felt safe and loved. Just writing about it makes me shiver all over with goosebumps.

Ché flipped a few pages.

January 28

Uncle Clete touches me. I told him to stop but he said he would hurt me if I tell. They all make fun of me. I told them about the voices and what they were telling me. They think I am crazy.

February 1

I went to the store and I saw B. He acted like he didn't know me as that hussy hugged him. She thinks she is something with those fancy hot pants and stuff. Ma'dear says she is going to hell for dressing like that. I can't believe he ignored me even though we had such a wonderful night. He comes to me almost every night now.

*   *   *

The pastor's deep laughter echoed loudly down the hall-way. Ché jumped. It sounded as if they had moved to the front door. Her pulse quickened as she closed the book. Why was her mother reading this over and over? As she placed the book back inside the box, an old newspaper clipping slipped out and fluttered to the ground. She hurriedly picked it up. It was slightly yellowed and felt brittle in her hands and she carefully unfolded it. It appeared to be a clipping from an old society page. "Chappee Weds," it said. Many of the words had yellowed and faded over time, and the small picture of a bride and groom was hard to see. She opened the old diary and carefully placed the clipping inside the back cover.

The front door was opening and the voices rose, saying good-bye. Ché snapped the small lock on the box closed and ran to her mother's bathroom, quickly opening the closet door. She wiped away the sweat that had broken out on her forehead.

Deborah walked into the bedroom. It only took her a minute to make her way to the walk-in closet. Ché was holding up a dress as if she were considering wearing it.

"Didn't I tell you to stay out of my things?" Deborah stood at the closet door with her hands on her hips.

"I need something to wear later, Ma." She paused.

Deborah stepped forward, shoving Ché backward as she grabbed the hanger from her daughter's hands.

"You have plenty in your own closet. I don't like it when you wear my clothes. You don't know how to treat fine things and you are shaped different than I am. You make hips in my clothes."

Ché rubbed her right shoulder. It hurt where her mother had pushed her. She could feel the imprint of her bony finger on her shoulder bone. Her mother looked tired and her hair appeared to be thinning.

"Everything okay, Ma?" she asked.

Deborah hung her dress back in its place.

"Everything's fine," she snapped. "And it will be much better when you remember to send your clothes to the cleaners."

Bill poked his head into the closet. "Is all the yelling necessary? You okay in here?"

Deborah forced a smile, her eyes like steel as her gaze remained fixed on her daughter.

Ché pushed past her mother, glad to be rescued. "I guess I'll find something else to wear." She avoided the pastor's gaze as she left the room and hurried down the hall, more confused than ever. Her mother had been right. There was obviously a lot she did not understand.

22

The doorbell rang promptly at eight o'clock. Although she was less than enthusiastic, Angelica felt her stomach move as the door chimed. She made one last attempt to smooth her hair back into its simple ponytail. That was easier said than done today. Her locks seemed to have a mind of their own.

The phone was ringing again, but Angelica ignored it. It was either Ché or Jeanette, and Angelica did not want to talk with either of them.

It had been hard to avoid Jeanette's questions. She had called four times in the past two days. Angelica knew she was curious, and she became even more so when Angelica avoided her questions. This seemed to be the only way to get things done and she did not want her friend to try and talk her out of it. It was best just not to tell her what she was planning. After she called the first time, Angelica avoided answering the phone.

The doorbell rang again. Her date was obviously impatient.

She glanced one last time into the mirror, then swung the door open.

Angelica was speechless. The man at the door was every bit as gorgeous as the picture in the ad. He was just a little taller than the six feet she asked for, and muscular, but still slender. She looked up into a face framed by sexy long hair, fashioned into perfectly groomed dreadlocks. This was good. No false advertising here. An herbal smell drifted past her nose. It wasn't overpowering, but warm, and it made her feel slightly more comfortable instantly.

He was clean-shaven, and his face had a certain rugged look that was attractive, but not pretty. His eyes were almond-shaped and he had sensual lips that he licked before he spoke.

"I'm not sure I'm in the right place," he said.

"Yes, yes, you are." Unconsciously, she smoothed her clothes, immediately regretting not paying more attention to how she was dressed.

"I'm Angelica. Come in," she said, stepping away from the door, making room for him to enter. She extended her hand for a handshake, but instead he took it in his own and raised it to his mouth. His lips barely brushed the back, suggesting a kiss that was more like a remnant of chivalrous days gone by than real. Angelica smiled, surprised.

"Will we be dining out?" he asked.

Angelica laughed, suddenly more confident. "Is eating required?"

"No, we can do whatever you want. Aren't you a little young to need an escort?"

"Is there an age requirement?" She tilted her head to the side, lifting her eyebrows at the same time. She could play this game. Make-believe cat-and-mouse. "Would you like something to drink?" she asked. Got to remember those southern manners.

"No, there is no age requirement," he said. "It's just that most of my clients are older ladies. I'll have a diet Coke, if you have any."

She headed toward the kitchen. "That seems to be a popular drink these days." She was thinking of her last encounter with the Good Samaritan who returned her wallet. "You watching your figure?"

Her guest followed her instead of sitting. He threw his head back and laughed easily. His luxurious mane flowed about his shoulders. "I hope that isn't a disappointment."

A thought suddenly occurred to Angelica. Maybe she would fare better if she was just frank, straight out.

"Look, I hired you for one thing, and one thing only. I am a virgin." She paused, looking for some sort of emotion or reaction on her escort's face. She handed him the Coke. "What did you say your name was?"

"John," He said. "We are all named John." He didn't smile or otherwise show any emotion. "Most people hire us for one thing only. I don't understand why you would need to hire anyone at all. For anything." He looked Angelica up and down. "You're young and cute. There are probably a hundred guys that would love to go out with you."

"That is not your concern. You are here strictly because I want to lose my virginity. Now." *There*. It was out. It crossed her mind that this might be illegal. She hadn't even thought to check.

The room was still, and they were both so silent that the sounds of their breathing seemed to echo throughout the kitchen.

"Oh," he said. "I guess that means there will be no dinner." He grinned.

Angelica felt relief. It was the first hint of emotion that had come out of him since he walked through the door. The atmosphere in the room was suddenly lighter. She looked at him and grinned back, from ear to ear. "You surprised?"

"No, I get all kinds of strange requests. But I still think you might like it better if I was someone you were dating or something."

"I told you not to worry about that. Can you handle it?"

He laughed again. "It's your money, honey. Don't I need to be asking you that question, Angelica?"

Angelica could not help feeling that the glint in his eyes hid a big secret. She shuddered. "Why do you do this?" she asked.

"This? You mean escort? It pays the bills. I'm a student. I guess it's equivalent to women who table dance for money to pay tuition. I escort."

"But table dancing is different. Most of those girls don't—"

"Don't what? Have sex? Have you ever been a table dancer? Do you know that? And who said that is what I do? I escort ladies for money, not have sex with them. Now, of course, if that happens while I am escorting . . ."

"I see." Angelica looked down at the floor. She was a little bit disappointed with his reasons. "Don't you get tired of it?"

John laughed. "Why should I get tired? It's an easy job and many of my clients don't want me to sleep with them. They really do need an escort to dinner or something. And I have regulars. I get paid where other guys are begging."

"Don't you worry about disease? You can't be too careful."

"I protect myself. I have a selection of condoms right here." He patted his breast pocket. "I even have female condoms. Those take a little practice. I don't think you're ready for those." He winked. This time they both laughed.

"If you're hungry, I could feed you. I wasn't planning on it, but I could whip together something."

"Look, it's your money. I get paid by the hour, remember? It doesn't matter whether you are cooking in the kitchen or standing here looking at me." He looked around the rooms and rubbed the palms of his hands together. "Well, do you want to go at it right here in the living room? I think I would like to make it nice for you. Can we move to the bedroom?"

Angelica shrugged. "I guess the bedroom would be better." She might as well get down to business. The sooner, the better. "Come on." Angelica stood up uneasily and signaled for John to follow.

"Wait," he said as they passed through the kitchen. "Do you have any candles? Any wine?"

Relief once again flooded over Angelica. Tension had been building up. He was trying to make the situation have at least some semblance of normalcy. "Sure. Let me get them. Anything else?"

"Wineglasses." He winked.

"Thanks." Angelica was glad that he understood, or at least seemed to.

He caressed her face. She moved closer, involuntarily. She liked it, and she was scared. This was far stranger than she ever imagined it would be a week ago. Angelica felt lost. A hug that meant something would be nice.

"No thanks needed. I want satisfied customers. Repeat business is important."

Angelica pointed him toward the bedroom as she went in search of the glasses, wine, and candles. Although she knew John was trying to make her comfortable, she felt the familiar nervousness begin to set in once again. No matter what, it still didn't feel quite right. By now she had learned that it wasn't over until it was over. Things still could go wrong.

By the time she reached the bedroom, he was sitting on the sofa there, and he stood up, meeting her and taking the things from her hands.

"You get comfortable," he said. He placed the candles on the nightstands on either side of Angelica's wrought-iron bed, then lit them with matches he took from his pocket. Angelica, now sitting on the sofa, watched silently, with her legs crossed. One of them bounced up and down quickly, involuntarily.

John opened the wine and turned and winked. "You okay?"

"Yeah, I'm fine," she lied. He was attempting to make her more comfortable, that she knew, but the slow and deliberate way he moved was not sexy to Angelica. Instead, it made her more and more nervous. She kept stealing glances at her watch. She felt his meter, her money, and her nerve ticking away.

John removed his jacket. Angelica swallowed, trying to push her uneasiness away. She could hear her watch as if it were a grandfather clock.

"Would you like some music? Would that make you more comfortable?" He knelt before her on the floor and ran his smooth hands up and down the length of her arms. She shook her head.

"Okay, you're the boss," he said.

Angelica was speechless as she watched him stand up and begin to take off his shirt. He unbuttoned each button carefully. Angelica felt as if she were watching a well-rehearsed strip-tease. He removed the shirt, then his undershirt, and reached for his belt. Instead of becoming excited, Angelica felt herself trying to melt back into the sofa, wishing she could fall through it, into a different place and time.

John removed his pants and Angelica's eyes came to rest on his underwear, a thong. She blinked. He appeared rather large. Was there a sock in there or something? Maybe the candlelight was playing tricks on her, like the supermarket lighting had before. She had mistaken the other guy she met in the supermarket for a nice single guy, and instead she got a lecher. Now, that was funny. Who was being the lecherous one now?

Angelica's eyes were riveted to John's crotch. Any thoughts of smiling vanished quickly. The hairs on her arms prickled from the emotional chill. John hesitated in a way that suggested that he thought he was exciting his client, teasing her.

"You ready?" His voice was low, almost whispering.

Angelica didn't move. She couldn't. His performance had turned her to stone as if she were staring Medusa in the face. She was riveted.

Slowly, John removed his underwear. He turned and placed it on the bed carefully, bending over so that Angelica could get a full view of his well-rounded, muscular behind.

He turned back around in slow motion. Angelica gasped. John was equipped with the largest penis she had ever seen. He could have starred in one of those porn movies that Jeanette's parents watched. He reached down, taking himself in his hands.

"You like?" he said.

Angelica was without words. It was unreal. He stepped toward her.

"No." She sank farther back into the sofa, putting her hands up in front of her. "I've changed my mind. I don't think so."

John paused, placing his hand on his well-formed hip. He was no longer smiling. "You do know that I get paid whether we do or don't, right? It's no sweat off my back."

"You're too . . . " She couldn't finish her sentence. The phone rang and Angelica grabbed it. There was no way in hell he was touching her with *that* thing. She would be bruised internally for sure.

"Jeanette!" she said, her voice full of false enthusiasm.

John stood directly in front of her, his hands on his hips.

"Can I call you back? I need to take a shower." Angelica pictured the day they had secretly watched those videos together. It was an accident, the tapes were unmarked. They were looking for some tapes of *Soul Food*. They had laughed for days. "I'll call back, just give me about an hour. Okay?" She hung up the phone.

"Look, I understand. It's your call. But I can be gentle. I'm very experienced." John grabbed his clothing and began to dress himself. "I'll tell you what. How about we start over? Just go to hear some music. No pressure." He was smiling again.

Angelica glanced at her watch. She cocked her head to the side. If she wasn't going to get what she originally needed, why should she pay? What was the use?

John seemed to sense her thoughts. "Angelica. Off the clock. Just the basic fee that you already owe. It's between us, okay?" He continued dressing.

Angelica felt herself relax once again. He seemed to be a really nice guy. Why he was doing this type of work was beyond her. She might as well go. Anything was better than staying around the house feeling sorry for herself. She was running out of time. She had no inheritance and no money to give to the church. Ché would surely spread rumors around and she had nothing to show for it. Maybe she should just move away and forget it.

She looked at John and nodded. "Just let me straighten up and change my clothes. Is your name really John?"

He shook his head. "No, it's not. It's Marcus."

They laughed. "Well, thanks Marcus. It's nice to meet you. I'll be ready in ten."

23

There weren't that many people at the jazz club when Juan and James arrived. Juan surveyed the room. People didn't overpower it. The music was mellow, just what he needed to relax.

"Want a drink, man? It's on me." James tapped Juan on his shoulder. "Why don't you find us a place to sit? You want a soda?" He grinned.

"Make fun if you want, man. Alcohol is going to kill you one day."

"Not before coffee kills you. Besides, you gotta go somehow, Jefe, right?" James raised his eyebrows.

"Yeah, that's true, but you need to treat your body like the temple it is."

James laughed. "Don't give me that, man. When was the last time you worked out or anything? At least I work off all my drink in the dojo. Not an ounce of fat on me." He patted his stomach.

The two friends made their way to the front of the room, right outside the reach of the spotlight centered on the stage. Juan pulled out a chair. "I want a diet Coke. Think you can handle that, man?"

"Barely. You don't pay me enough. Do you think you can handle it? You know those diet Cokes can be potent."

James grinned again as he walked to the bar to get the drinks. Juan sat at the table, intent on listening to the music. He wanted to focus, prepare for his performance. Instead he found his mind wandering back to the girl he had seen at the newsstand. He could not seem to shake the feeling that he'd seen her before somewhere, but he could not place her. The vision of her haunted him.

"Juan, are you daydreaming again? What's up? If I didn't know better, I would think you had a girl on your mind. Anyway, listen up. David wants to know if you brought your sax. He wants you to play a little. I didn't want to tell him that it was always in the car. I didn't know if you were in the mood." He placed the glasses he was carrying down on the table.

"Seriously? You wouldn't kid me, would you?" Juan sat far forward in his chair. James was always looking out for him.

"Naw, man, I know how serious you are about that horn. So, you down, or what?" James paused. He already knew Juan would say yes.

"Say no more. You know I am always prepared. I'll be right back." Juan jumped up from the table and headed toward the door. Music already flowed through his head. James turned toward the bar, making eye contact with the gentleman behind it. He raised one hand and gave him the thumbs-up sign. He didn't agree with the way his friend was treating his father, but he loved to hear him play.

24

Angelica pulled into the parking lot behind Marcus. The building in front of them was unmarked, no name on the door at all. Angelica glanced around, not recognizing the place. The parking lot was filled with several late-model cars. She sat in her car, waiting.

Marcus opened his door and approached Angelica's car. She opened the window and allowed him to lean in.

"Um, this ain't no freaky strip club or anything, is it? I heard about what goes on in some of those places. Just because I called an escort service doesn't mean I'm into that type of thing." Her voice was almost edgy.

"Relax. This is a nice place. Jazz. Real mellow. People can talk here, chill out. I come here all the time. The live music is nice."

"I haven't really been into jazz," Angelica said, wrinkling her nose. Remembering the last time she was in the jazz room at Bakari and her first-date-gone-bad brought a bad taste to her mouth.

"Then now is a good time to start. Sometimes the music really helps me get my head together. Seems to me you could use a little of that. If you don't like it, you can leave. Isn't that why we drove separate cars?" He opened the door and held it for Angelica to exit. "You better close your window."

Angelica rolled up the window. This was probably for the better. She stepped out of the car.

"Well, my Pop-pop used to always put jazz music on when he wanted to think. Maybe it will put me in a thinking place, too. I do have a few things to sort out." Marcus extended his arm and she took it.

"I can tell that. You just don't seem like the escort service type." He smiled.

"That's 'cause I'm not." Angelica smiled a little for the first time since they left the house. Maybe if she acted normal, like this was an ordinary date, things would turn out all right after all.

They walked toward the door of the club arm in arm. As they were about to step inside, someone pushed past them at the door, carrying an instrument case. Angelica stumbled.

"Well, he was certainly in a hurry," Marcus said. He took her elbow to steady her as she stepped aside.

Angelica shrugged. "Looks like he's in the band or something. Maybe he was late."

"Maybe. But 'excuse me' would have been nice."

She let Marcus pay the cover. No one bothered to ask her for identification this time. They seemed to know Marcus, and Angelica followed his lead. They were led to a small table, not too far from the front of the room. Marcus pulled out the chair and motioned for Angelica to sit. She smiled. He was trained to be a gentleman. It was how he made his living, but it was still nice.

A waiter came over and took their drink orders. Angelica shook her head. Although she had not been asked for identification, she was not willing to take a chance on ordering a drink, and she agreed to come here to clear her head, not get it fogged up. She'd already imbibed far too much wine over the past couple of days anyway, and it certainly hadn't helped.

She looked around the club. It wasn't a bad spot. A few round tables, low lights. A small crowd of people. It was intimate.

The lights dimmed, making it difficult to see much past the closest two or three tables. She narrowed her eyes to try and make out the features of the people around her. Everyone seemed to be so mellow. Angelica was getting an education about the nightclub scene this week, for sure.

She made eye contact with a man at one table, not far from where she was seated. He raised his glass in her direction and smiled. Angelica turned away.

Someone walked onto the stage. He raised his saxophone to his lips. He seemed familiar . . . very familiar. She gasped, drawing in her breath sharply. She was staring at the guy that was in the uniform the first night, in the revolving door at the hotel. Marcus noticed her reaction and looked in her direction. She closed her eyes, then opened them again. He wasn't a dream. He was still gorgeous. He still had the glow she remembered from that night. Angelica put her hand on her stomach in an attempt to calm the butterflies. It was as if she were in the middle of her own sappy love story.

Marcus touched her arm. "You okay? You look flushed."

She nodded, only vaguely aware that Marcus had spoken.

The man on the stage started to play and Angelica remained transfixed. He was fabulous. Angelica knew there was something special about him, even before he played a note. Marcus looked at her, then at the saxophone player, and then back at Angelica again. The way she looked at the man on the stage told him that Angelica was lost in the music he played.

25

Juan took a moment to stand behind the curtain before going through it. He wanted to wow this crowd. He took a breath and raised his eyes, quickly asking for blessings and free-flowing creativity. He stepped through the curtain and into the spotlight. There was a smattering of polite applause. He waited for a couple that had just been seated in front to finish giving their drink orders to their waiter. He looked at the floor while they did.

There were a few rumbles in the room as people began to get uneasy that he was not playing. He was going to change that. Blow them all away. Juan raised his saxophone to his lips and momentarily closed his eyes.

He had not expected to get a chance to play tonight. He was so excited, he'd almost knocked over a couple in the doorway coming back from his car. He opened his eyes, making eye contact with some people near the front. He still had not played a note. Showmanship was half the game and he wanted to build up anticipation in the crowd.

His eyes came to rest on a table right in front, and he almost lost his concentration. He dropped his arms back down to his sides. The girl from the newsstand was sitting there, staring right at him. She was even more remarkable than she'd been earlier in the day. He again lifted his sax to his mouth, and began to blow. What he'd planned to play while he was back stage left him, and he just played from his heart. He barely heard the sounds he made.

He played to her. He knew he was playing the most remarkable performance of his life, and probably could never do it again. He wanted to make her see what he felt through his notes. All attention was on him.

He was done when he was done. He just stopped and never finished the song; he simply abandoned it after he poured his heart into the message. The crowd in the room was on its feet, clapping for him, but the sound was muted in his head. She was all he could see, and he was only vaguely aware that she was with someone.

He finally realized that he was finished as the applause began to die out. Juan bowed slightly to the crowd. He walked off the stage, noticing that the man with the woman nudged her slightly. She ignored him and smiled at Juan.

James met him backstage, grinning. "That was great!" He slapped Juan on the back. "You have some serious talent!"

Juan stood there, seemingly paralyzed. He finally nodded.

"You are too hard on yourself, man. You were really good."

Juan licked his lips. "She's here."

"Who?" James looked confused. "Don't tell me. You had another vision, right? Someone caught your eye in the audience?"

"Not someone. That girl that I told you about. The one I saw earlier today. She's here, right down front."

Juan was in a trance, his eyes glazed over. He nodded his head as James shook him.

"So, are you going to go and talk to her or what? You always talking about how you are the mack daddy and stuff, Jefe."

Juan knew that this was his chance. He'd been given two in one twenty-four-hour period; it must have been meant to be.

He frowned. "But she seems to be with someone."

"Well, that never presented a problem to you before. I don't see anything wrong with you going over there and introducing yourself. It would be like mingling with the crowd, know what I mean?" James poked Juan with his elbow and winked.

James was right. What did he have to lose? James left him and headed back out to the tables, patting him on the back like a father would.

Juan removed his reed from his saxophone and placed it back in its case. Someone was definitely trying to tell him something. It was obviously meant for him to meet that young lady, for whatever reason. He walked from behind the stage over to where James now sat nursing his drink. Juan placed his hand on James's back. He waited for him to say something smart like he always did, but this time James just nodded and pushed him a little, his hands encouraging Juan to make a move.

Juan placed his instrument case on the floor and picked up his diet Coke. He swigged it like there was something special in that soda that could give him more courage than he seemed to have at the moment. He smoothed his shirt.

What was the deal? He'd never found himself at a loss for words before when it came to a woman, but then again, no young lady had ever stopped time in his presence, either. Even dust seemed to stop moving. He shook his head. Juan could not think of one smart line to say.

He smiled, turned around, and walked purposefully toward her. What would this guy she was with do? Juan wasn't sure he cared and he was willing to take the chance. He paused behind her chair and the man with her looked up at him.

She turned around, and Juan drew in his breath. He stuttered at first.

"H-h-hey. Thanks for coming out. Did you enjoy the music?"

She stared at him and nodded. Her friend extended his hand.

"You were great. I'm Marcus. This is Angelica." With that, Marcus stood, excusing himself.

"May I sit?" Juan said. Angelica nodded, seeming only now to notice that Marcus was gone. "I think he went to the restroom or something. I hope I didn't chase him away."

Angelica finally spoke. "No problem. We're just friends—acquaintances, really." She immediately felt as if she'd said too much. Did he ask her for any information like that? Her faced flushed with embarrassment.

"Okay. That's good, then," he said.

"I've seen you before." Angelica and Juan both started to speak at the same time. They smiled, then laughed at themselves.

Juan motioned that she should speak first. The awkwardness between them lightened, and she sat back in her chair for the first time since she'd spotted Juan on the stage.

"I saw you at the Hilton a day or so ago. In the revolving door. You were delivering some things. I didn't think you saw me."

"I didn't. I saw you at a newsstand, near that big church. That was earlier today."

Angelica tapped on the table, playing with her keys in her hand. She looked down at them. Did he see what she had bought, too? Could he tell what her purpose had been? "Near Lost Pilgrim? Talk about coincidence!" She smiled.

"Life is full of coincidences waiting to happen."

"So, are you moonlighting as a musician? You make deliveries for a living?" She felt her face get hot again and she raised her hand to her cheek.

Juan was both mesmerized and delighted by her smile. "No, I think I was moonlighting as a delivery person. Music is my first love."

"Really? Mine, too. I want to be a singer."

"Want to be?" he said.

"Yeah. I don't actually sing anywhere yet, other than the choir sometimes. I do take a few classes at the music school here, but no big deal. But I know there is a singer inside me. I want to go to a professional music school. To Juilliard." Angelica again felt as if she were spilling her life story to this stranger.

Juan looked surprised. "Juilliard? That's in New York. The big time. I'm from there. I'm just in town for a little while. Working in the family business."

Angelica didn't have time to answer. Marcus was back, standing next to Juan. He cleared his throat.

Juan looked around the room quickly, hoping to spot James. He always seemed to barge in—why couldn't he do that now, maybe intercepting Marcus before he had a chance to return?

Although they were aware of Marcus, Angelica and Juan kept their eye contact. Marcus could sense that he was not welcome. Juan and Angelica were silent now, and seemed to be waiting for him to excuse himself again.

"Angelica, I just got a page. Duty calls."

She looked up. "Right, okay."

Marcus put his hand on hers and their eyes met for a moment. An unspoken thank-you passed from Angelica to Marcus while Juan looked on. There was only so much of her business this handsome stranger needed to know. She was not about to leave. Something felt right for her for the first time in about a week. She reached down for her purse. She did have to pay Marcus.

He stopped her. "No, it's on me, okay?"

Angelica smiled.

"You going to be okay?" Marcus asked. Angelica nodded, and after a quick nod to Juan, Marcus emptied his glass and made his exit.

Juan wondered what the exchange between Angelica and Marcus was about, but decided it really didn't matter.

"I hope I wasn't interrupting anything."

"No, you are fine. We just wanted to hear a little music, that's all."

Juan found himself feeling surprisingly at ease. He was sitting with the most beautiful creature he'd ever seen in his life, and he was positive the beauty he was seeing was not all physical. It was much more than that. Angelica was not from New York, not from the Caribbean, and not from Puerto Rico, so his father might not agree, but Juan knew that she was wife material. He felt that in his heart.

The feeling was mutual for Angelica. As far as she was concerned, they were the only people in the bar. For the first time since she'd found out what she had to do to gain her inheritance, she felt completely and totally at ease, too. For that short moment, there was nothing in the world to worry about.

26

The church parking lot was busy as always. Both Deborah and Ché knew it would be. The main church choir was going to be in the semifinals, so they were continuing to rehearse and the church trustee meeting was scheduled for tonight, too.

Ché looked over at her mother behind the wheel of the car. She seemed withdrawn, worried. She seemed to become more and more troubled as the week wore on. Ché had yet to make sense of the diary or the newspaper clipping. She wished she'd had more time to look through the things in the box. She was sure there were more clues in there, but she could never get close enough to it. Her mother had moved it, almost as if she'd suspected what Ché had done.

"Everything okay, Ma?" she asked, though she already knew what her mother would say.

"Fine. It will be fine." Deborah said. She drove past the parking space normally reserved for her. It was already taken. She pressed her lips together to try and contain her annoyance.

"Don't they see the sign? It says RESERVED FOR DEBORAH DAVIS, plain as day. Last time I checked, that was me." She let out her breath in disgust. This was just another sign of disrespect from the church members.

"Ma, this trustee thing. You know we can just leave, right? I really don't—"

Deborah's head snapped around. "No, Ché, you really don't understand. Haven't I told you that this time it's different?"

Ché recoiled from her mother. Deborah was becoming unpredictable. She made her voice small. "Ma, it's not like this is the first time that people thought something was going on. At that other church, we just left when it happened. We could do that now, right? You know that this is risky. Someone might really start probing around. Find out that—"

"I don't care if they know. So what if they do? We ain't really married. He doesn't know that, not yet. Besides, I really don't care about the little bit of church money. This time it's bigger than that."

Her mother's actions made this obvious. Two churches ago, her mother finally explained to her why they moved around so much from place to place, why she married so often. At first Ché was shocked to find out about her mother's elaborate scheme to make a living, but she began to accept it.

Deborah married single pastors and played perfect

church wife for a while. Made him comfortable, skimmed a little money, and then she and Ché would move on before anyone was wiser. It seemed far-fetched at first, but it seemed to work. Ché found out a while ago that Deborah's last foster father, the one who wanted to send her away, was a minister, too. There was obviously some connection, but she couldn't put her finger on that, either. And as far as Ché knew, her mother had only paid someone off once to be quiet. It was amazing what could be overlooked if the right palms were greased, and lonely people always wanted to believe they were loved.

As long as Deborah married the pastor of a large church, it was okay, not a bad deal. Ché couldn't complain; she always got everything she wanted with no problem. She always had more spending money than all of her friends. This last time, Ché even helped Deborah find Bill and his church. She was the one to find his pitiful Internet classified ad looking for a churchgoing woman, or so she thought. She should have known it was almost too easy; the page with the ad on it had been printed out with others Ché had been told to go through.

Deborah fit what Bill was looking for almost exactly. He even asked for a woman much younger than he, and her mother seemed determined this last time to find someone in or near this part of Louisiana. He was old enough to be her father, but he appeared happy as he ran around taking care of Deborah's every need. At first Ché was annoyed, almost disgusted, but she soon grew to like him, as he doted on her, too.

NINA FOXX

Deborah was moving her lips again, with no real sound coming out, like she was talking to herself. Ché frowned. She'd never done that before, no matter how tense things got.

"What was that, Ma?" Ché asked.

"Nothing. I wasn't talking to you, girl. You ready for this meeting? I need to go to help Bill. I'm not sure he can handle this. This situation needs to be contained until that Chappee girl—"

It could be another million years and Ché knew she would never understand her mother. "Contained? Situation? Ma, I swear you are losing it. What the hell are you talking about? And why are you so concerned about Angelica?"

Deborah took one hand off the steering wheel and slapped Ché on the side of her head with so much force, her head hit the side window. Deborah swerved to avoid a light pole and Ché reached up with both hands, grabbing her head. She was more startled than hurt. She was numb.

"Ma, why?" Ché could not remember a time when her mother was mad enough her to hit her like that. She had not meant to be disrespectful, she just wanted her mother to fill her in on more of the details. She was getting too old to be treated like she was a child.

"I thought I told you never to swear at me, girl!" Deborah yelled, sounding almost desperate. Her left eye started twitching. "Didn't I tell you *I* am the mother here? That means you do what I say and respect me until you get out of my house. You don't seem to understand how important this is!"

Ché opened her mouth to speak, but Deborah cut her off.

"Don't." She held up her hand and motioned for Ché to stop. "Listen, I have worked very hard to make sure that you don't experience the things I had to, growing up in all kinds of foster homes." Her voice softened as she pulled into a parking space farther back in the lot.

Ché whimpered. She hoped she would not bruise. She opened and closed her mouth, making sure her jaw still worked. Her mother sure packed a wallop. But this irrational behavior was new. Even her crazy schemes used to have a method embedded in them. Not anymore. Nothing made sense now.

Deborah turned off the car and continued. "Remember when I told you that I was entitled to that money and that there were things here that you didn't know about? This started well before you were born, even before I was born." She paused.

Ché looked at her mother with renewed interest.

"You don't know anything about my mother, your grandmother, do you? Do you know why that is?" Deborah said.

Ché shook her head. She often wondered about her mother's family. Deborah never mentioned them, and only occasionally would she refer to her life in foster care.

"My mother killed herself because of that man. Right after I was born. Everything bad about my life is his fault." Her voice was low and filled with disdain. She spoke as if she were talking about some dreaded disease rather than a person they both had known. Her whole body trembled,

filled with hate. She looked down at her lap, almost relieved, as if she had just let some deep, dark secret out of
the closet.

Ché did not know what to say. Was she talking about Angelica's grandfather? She suddenly understood why her
mother thought she was entitled to the money, any money
from the Chappee family. She wanted reparations. But how
had it happened? Reparations for what? Ché could only
wonder. She was afraid to push any further.

Deborah seemed to read her thoughts. "I'll have to tell you
the whole story later. It's a miracle that even I know the truth.
Bill Chappee died before I could get more proof. All I have is
a letter my mother wrote to me before she died. She jumped
out of a hospital window, right after she had me." Deborah
dabbed at the corners of her eyes, stopped any tears from
rolling. And opened her car door. "Here comes Betty. It's
time for the meeting." Deborah began to get out of the car.

Ché got out, too, making eye contact with her mother.
She searched her face, but saw no remnants of the wild-
looking person who had slap-punched her in the car.

Deborah was already slipping back into her "beauty pageant" face and smile as she greeted Sister Betty. Ché
touched her cheek gingerly and shook her head.

Sister Betty finally left them in the lobby. Everyone having
said their hellos, Deborah and Ché walked into the meeting
together. Deborah held Ché's hand as if she felt bad for having struck her earlier. Ché could feel her apology without
her having to say a word.

"Ma, don't worry," she said. "I think Angelica Chappee will make her intentions known tonight. I know she will." She tightened her grip on her mother's hand.

"I hope you're right," Deborah said.

Ché shuddered. It sounded as if her mother was really being pushed to the edge. She was becoming more and more distant, like she never was before, and that was frightening. Deborah was all Ché had. In her state of mind, Ché didn't doubt that Deborah was capable of doing some extremely evil things. She just hoped the target of her actions would be someone other than herself.

Deborah fidgeted throughout the whole trustee meeting. Bill did not seem to be able to stand up for himself, no matter how much help she gave him. Instead of asserting himself like she wanted, he kowtowed to the trustees every chance he got, trying to avoid the blame for the money he deemed was somehow misplaced by an accounting faux pas. Couldn't he think of a better excuse than that?

"No, you may be right, Brother Young. I have not been as diligent as I need to be." Bill bowed his head and nodded, his hands clasped in front of him. Several of the attendees were glowering at him.

"No, Pastor, you haven't been. You been too busy with that young wife of yours. Sometimes when folks ain't your own people, they can turn you away from the issues at hand. You know, when we get old we want to be young again. You been tending to your midlife crisis instead of business."

Deborah was disgusted with Bill as she watched him let

these smelly old men push him around. He didn't even stand up for her when they were taking obvious shots at her and her character. He did not appear to know how to change the subject, start some action. He was at a loss to know what he should do. Couldn't he tell he needed to do something other than just deny that he had any knowledge? Why didn't he make something up? This obviously wasn't working. Soon people would start to investigate, ask personal questions, and that meant about her, too. They might find out that their marriage was not valid, that she had never divorced her first husband.

Ché paid almost no attention to the meeting. Instead, she kept looking toward the door, wondering where Angelica was. Hadn't she made herself clear at her little "visit"? Angelica seemed to be so shocked during their conversation, Ché was sure she was going to come running through the door at any minute, probably with her checkbook in her hand. Ché did not think her mother could take it if she didn't; she wasn't sure she could take her mother's reaction if she didn't. Deborah seemed about to snap. Ché didn't want her mother to have any reason to think that she was not doing what she'd asked her to do.

Deborah twitched in her sit and murmured constantly. Ché was unable to follow the meeting and unable to stand her mother's constant torment. If she watched Deborah reapply makeup one more time, she would puke. Ché excused herself. She had to go and call Angelica. Perhaps that would be enough to get her moving in the right direction, in the *giving* direction.

Ché dialed Angelica's number, got the answering machine, and hung up. She dialed the number again. She meant business, and Angelica needed to know that, too.

Ché did not know all the details about her grandmother, and she was sure there was more to the story than her mother had told her. Angelica didn't need to know that, though. All she needed to know was that Ché had more ammunition that she could use to turn up the pressure. She had to; her mother was all she had in her life.

27

Angelica heard the phone ring, but she didn't answer. The only thing on her mind tonight was Juan. They'd spent most of last evening together, on the phone, talking. He had called her almost as soon as she walked through the door. Angelica felt as if she knew him forever, as if he were an old friend that she needed to catch up with.

She shivered. Her fingertips were wrinkled and her bathwater had cooled to lukewarm. It was time to get out of the perfumed water and get dressed. Angelica was relaxed and at ease, her mind no longer on the recent drama. Nothing seemed so urgent anymore.

She wrapped herself in a large white towel. She sighed; white was the only color towel her grandfather would use, so that was all they had in the house. Although she couldn't get Juan out of her mind, everything reminded her of her grandfather. Even how she met Juan reminded her of the stories her grandfather had told her about him being young and romantic. He seemed to have been quite the ladies' man. Maybe that was why he was so protective of her. Angelica finished drying herself. Pop-pop wasn't irrational about her, though. He was protective, but not overly so. He always cautioned her about getting caught up in the moment and doing things she would regret. He taught her to think about the consequences of her actions before she took them, and always reminded her to use good common sense. There was nothing about his current challenge that fit in with that belief.

She moved into her bedroom, taking the candle that was burning during her bath with her. The scent of vanilla and sandalwood proved to be especially relaxing, as Juan had suggested it would be, and Angelica wanted to prolong its effect on her as long as possible. She did not choose a sexy outfit or plan her underwear as she had for her other dates. Instead she chose a comfortable pair of jeans and a shirt. She knew clothes were not what would matter to Juan.

The clock by her bedside read seven P.M. Juan would be arriving in a few minutes. Angelica smiled and blew out her candle. She moved to the living room, Juan constantly on her mind. They had talked a lot last night, but she'd failed to mention any of her present troubles. She did not share with him that life as she knew it could quite possibly change drastically in just a few days. Besides, she wanted to be sure he really liked her before he knew about her family history. People did real strange things where money was involved.

She tried to read, but could not concentrate as she waited

for Juan. What would he think of her, or of her grandfather, when he found out what it would take for her to get her inheritance? He seemed so nice. Would he be able to understand and still respect her at all? Angelica did not feel like she wanted to keep secrets from Juan. She wanted him to be part of her life.

The doorbell interrupted her thoughts. She jumped. She rubbed her sweaty palms on her jeans and got up to answer the door. As she walked past the phone, the blinking indicator on the answering machine caught her eye. She decided to listen to the message so she wouldn't wonder what it was while she was with Juan. Ché's message was clear. If Angelica did not comply, she would do everything in her power to ruin the Chappee family name. It was a strange message. Angelica shrugged. Ché had gone from ruining her name to the Chappee family name, now. She didn't say how she would do that, just that she would.

Angelica opened the door, still frowning as the answering machine turned itself off.

"So, does this mean you're not happy to see me?" Juan greeted her, a bunch of flowers in his hand. But he let them drop to his side as soon as he saw Angelica's face. "Did I do something wrong already?"

Angelica shook her head and motioned for him to come in.

"I'm sorry. You didn't do anything. There is so much going on in my life that I don't know how to begin to explain to you," she said.

Juan felt immediately comfortable in Angelica's presence,

despite her obvious state of dismay. He followed her into the living room and sat down. He put the flowers down on the table, preparing himself for the worst.

Angelica wondered how much she should tell Juan. He could help her out, if he was willing. Angelica knew that more than anything else, she wanted respect from Juan. She felt they were meant to be friends. Withholding information to get what she wanted was not going to help a friendship grow between them. And the weight of having no one to share what she was going through was getting to be too much.

He didn't seem to be hurting for money, or to be a typical starving musician. Her inheritance might not be that big a deal to him. She looked at Juan waiting patiently, genuine concern reflected in his eyes.

She took a deep breath and decided to begin at the beginning.

"I told you that my grandfather just passed away, right?" She perched on the edge of the sofa.

Juan nodded.

"I found out that he owned a lot more than I was aware of. Quite a bit more. And he left everything to me." There. The words had spilled out of her mouth. It was all out on the table. Almost.

Juan waited. What was so bad about that? he wondered. He understood inheritances and birthrights. He was reminded of what his would be every day—that is, if he did what his father wanted. "Well, I don't see a problem there. You can do some of those things we talked about. Music school, travel. Move away from here. Maybe all of those things, right?"

"There is a condition. One I am having trouble understanding and completing. I have to lose my virginity by Sunday." She stared at Juan for a reaction. Angelica half expected him to get up and run out the door. Hearing it said aloud, it sounded like something from a bad television script, even to Angelica. And she had been living with it for days now.

Juan raised his hands. "Okay," he said. "TMI. Definitely, Too Much Information. More than I need or want to know." Flashbacks of Sabrina ran though his mind. Was there something about his personality that attracted women with issues? Did Angelica expect him to help her? Juan felt himself begin to withdraw. She was sharing much too easily. Angelica must have been too good to be true. But he decided to hear it all. "And the problem with that would be . . . ?"

"That I just can't get it together. I can't seem to . . ." Her voice trailed off.

Juan felt himself relaxed again. Angelica's forehead was furrowed. She was obviously struggling with this. "Can't seem to? Or don't want to? Maybe you're having a hard time because your heart just isn't in it," he said. This was something that Juan could relate to. His heart wasn't in his so-called family destiny, either. His heart had not really been with Sabrina.

Angelica paused. She knew Juan was right. "I just don't get why my grandfather would ask me to do such a thing. It seems the opposite of everything he believed in and taught me to believe." She sat down next to Juan.

"Well," he said, "have you thought about asking him?"

Angelica looked at Juan. Had he not heard her say her grandfather was dead? What the hell was he talking about?

Juan almost laughed at the perplexed look on Angelica's face. "What I'm trying to say is, it's okay to talk to him, even though he's gone. I believe that you can talk to those who came before you, you know. And sometimes they will help you find what you need, help guide you to the truth." He took Angelica's hand. "When your relatives die, become ancestors, do you really think they just abandon you?"

Angelica was silent, shaking her head. She searched Juan's face. He sat back, as if preparing to tell her a long story.

"When I was little, I used to laugh at my grandmother. I thought she was crazy. We all did. She refused to speak English and she kept to herself, like she had a lot of secrets she just was not willing to let out. She clung to the old ways like they were her lifeline. We didn't understand. She kept glasses of water on a shelf, along with little mementos and pictures. We kids were never allowed to touch them. And I certainly didn't get it, not for a long time.

"Every Monday, she would change that water and light candles there. I didn't understand until much later that what she was doing was her own way of thanking and communicating with those who had come before her. Not just her own mother and father and sister, who were all long gone, but her Indian, Spanish, and African ancestors, too. The water was symbolic; it was supposed to help nourish them on their journey, and in turn the ancestor would help and protect you. I came to respect and understand that, and her. She taught me that as long as you gave the ancestors their respect, they would never abandon you. She learned that from her mother, who learned it from hers."

"Sounds like physics applied to the afterlife to me," Angelica said. "It was one of my favorite subjects. Energy doesn't disappear, it changes form."

"Not physics. One of the basic principles of an African religion, carried on. That's all."

Under other circumstances, Angelica would have laughed at Juan. She wasn't really in the mood for a lesson on religion. But in her heart, she knew that she and her Pop-pop had been so close in life, there was no way he could ever abandon her. It made perfect sense.

The more she thought about it, the less it sounded like Juan was some kind of nut. Perhaps she should just go and try to talk to her grandfather, maybe try to sort things out in her own mind. Since the funeral, she had not really thought much about what she was being asked to do. She was so blinded by the money and what it meant, she just sat down and tried to figure out how to get it.

"W-well," she stammered, "I suppose I could just try and talk to him. I know people go and talk to graves all the time." She smiled, remembering warmly. "Pop-pop used to talk to the folks he was embalming, especially if he knew them before they died. He ran funeral homes."

"You could do the same, you know. And you don't have to go to his grave if you don't want to." Juan spoke gently. "If he was anything at all like you say, he would probably listen no matter where you chose to speak to him. Maybe it will help you understand what he was thinking when he structured his will the way he did. Know what I mean?"

Juan touched her hand again, gently. She'd been so upset when he arrived, he just wanted to protect her. He was putty around her and she didn't even know it. And he was supposed to be the mack daddy.

Angelica's trusting eyes were filled with confusion. She stood up and almost tripped over the coffee table. She went back to her bedroom, leaving Juan looking after her, confused.

"Angelica?" Juan raised his voice slightly, not knowing how far she had gone into the other parts of the house.

Finally he could hear her coming back toward him. She began talking before she reentered the living room.

"Sorry about that," she said. "I went to get the keys." Angelica held up a large ring of keys for Juan. "I know it's late, but do you think you can come with me?"

Juan wasn't sure what he was getting himself into, but there was something about Angelica that he knew he could trust. He stood up from the couch.

She smiled briefly at him, and he melted. He knew he would follow her to the ends of the earth. He reached out, drawing her close, and lowering his head to gently brush her neck with his lips. She smelled sweet and clean. He felt warmth rush through his body and he kissed her neck tenderly, hugging her closer. He was hooked.

28

Ché didn't even hear Deborah coming, and almost jumped out of her skin as she hung up the phone. She turned around, and her mother was standing right behind her, waiting.

"Well?" Deborah asked. She stood with one hand on her well-clothed hip. Ché was blocked from moving in any direction as Deborah stood, indignant, as if poised to kick Ché with one of her designer pumps if she so much as formed her mouth to say the wrong thing.

"Well, nothing, Ma." Ché remembered her mother's outburst in the car. She didn't want to provoke her again. The stormy look on her mother's face threw her off guard. She stammered, "I—I called Angelica. She wasn't there. I'd told her to come down here tonight, to the meeting. I thought for sure she was ready to make some kind of pledge to the church. Like you wanted." Ché moved as far back as she could, pressing against the phone, causing it to fall off the hook. It hit her on the back on the way down. She jumped.

"Things okay, ladies?" Mother Launders, one of the elder women in the church, interrupted them. The mood between them had been so intense, they'd overlooked the thump-click sound of her steel cane as she approached.

Ché nodded, and Deborah snapped her smile back into place so quickly, it took on more a sinister than a cheery look. She patted Ché's ropelike braids.

"Well, don't you let this church mess get you down, ya hear?" Mother Launders raised her cane in their direction. "I been around this here church so long, I seen lots of messes come and go. No use getting all in a huff about it. There was mess before you, there will be mess after you."

They were frozen as she twisted her jaw and used her mouth to adjust her dentures, nodding at them again. She waved, pausing to adjust her gray hair before she thump-clicked across the narthex and out the door.

They were silent until she left. Deborah stepped back away from Ché, relieving her of being sandwiched against the phone. She opened her purse and pulled out her compact. Deborah flipped it open, reapplying her makeup without looking in the mirror.

Ché looked on as that simple gesture appeared to help her mother pull herself back together, almost hiding the strange look that had been on her face just a minute earlier. She waited for Deborah to drop the compact back into her purse and stepped forward toward the doorway just as soon as she did.

Deborah grabbed her daughter's upper arm, stopping her in her tracks. "Wait," she said.

Ché froze, almost expecting her mother to hit her again.

Deborah looked over her shoulder, surveying the now-empty church vestibule.

"You're still my baby, right?" Her voice was so meek that Ché strained to hear her words. She looked at her mother, confused.

"I just need to know that you are still with me, honey." She released her viselike grip and gently rubbed Ché's arm.

Ché nodded. The wild look was there in her mother's eyes again. She was obviously losing it. One minute she loved Ché, the next she was blaming her for her lot in life. Ché didn't understand her at all.

They began to walk toward the door carefully, as if walking on ice. Ché was afraid to speak. The sooner this was over, the better.

"I'll go get the car." Deborah picked up speed and motioned for Ché to wait for her at the door. Ché gladly stopped. There were people in the parking lot and it wouldn't be hard for them to see the disturbed look on her face. There was no way in the world she could hide how she was feeling as well as her mother could.

She waited and worried. Why had Angelica decided not to come? Perhaps her threats were as not effective as she had thought they were. Maybe she read Angelica wrong. What would happen if Angelica didn't give money to the church like her mother wanted? Would Deborah do something stupid and get caught doing it? And what would happen to Ché if she did?

A car approached, and Ché looked up, expecting to see her mother. Instead, the car did not slow down near the doorway. As it got closer, Ché recognized it immediately. She felt her heart begin to beat harder. It was Angelica Chappee. For a split second, she was ecstatic, then disappointed as the car left the parking lot as if it had made a wrong turn. Ché craned her neck, stepping out into the parking lot to follow Angelica's car. It rounded the corner, moving out of Ché's sight.

Deborah made her way back to her car. She opened the door and let herself fall into the seat. Her heart beat heavily and she turned and placed her head down on the steering wheel. She had to get hold of herself. Everything seemed to be getting so overwhelming.

She reached out and closed her car door, taking a deep breath. She put the key in the ignition and then paused. She reached over to the passenger seat where she had placed her purse and opened it. Her fingers quickly found what she wanted. The letter she had placed there earlier was still safe and sound.

It was still in its original envelope, creased and yellowed with age. Deborah cherished the letter her mother had written her before she died, ever since it was given to her on her eighteenth birthday. She licked her lips and opened the envelope carefully, being sure not to tear the paper further. It had thinned and frayed over the years and the words were faded. Deborah stared at the paper in her trembling hands. She did not need to read it; she had committed the words to memory years ago.

She imagined herself greeting her true father and then embracing him. She'd known all her life that he would be glad to see her. She had committed herself to tracking him down, just like her mother said in the letter, so they could be together. She knew there would be a reason that he had not come for her. He had to know about her. There was no way he could not make the connection that his secret love affair with her mother had left behind a child. Maybe he had searched for her, too, not realizing that she had shown up right under his nose.

Salty tears found their way to her mouth and she used the back of her hand to wipe them away. The streetlight came on above her car and she blinked. She'd finally found him, but had waited too late. Not only had he not come to find her, but he hadn't acknowledged her, not even in his death. Instead he left all his money to some girl he wasn't even related to, not really, not by blood. That girl he married was pregnant when he'd met her, and he married her anyway.

"Angelica's mother wasn't even his. Damn hussy," Deborah sniffed. He was so good-hearted, he raised someone else's child. So why had he not searched for his own? Everyone in the church knew the truth, and she read it in her mother's diary. Angelica's grandmother must have been the "hussy" referred to in her mother's diary.

She replaced the letter in the side pocket in her bag. Then

she flipped down the visor and checked her makeup again, repairing the damage her tears had made. She pursed her lips, even more determined to get what was rightfully hers. No one would have believed the diary of the fifteen-year-old girl who had been her mother. The time for gathering more proof was past. Blood was thicker than water and she was going to prove it.

29

"Slow down. You went the wrong way." Angelica laughed. She playfully tapped Juan on the shoulder. "I meant turn at the corner, not at the church. If I knew you drove like this, I would have driven myself."

Juan turned the car around, leaving the parking lot at Lost Pilgrim.

"If you gave directions better, then I would have turned at the right place anyway," he said. He couldn't help laughing. He'd followed the directions Angelica was giving him step by step. She was good at being a backseat driver, and he felt like they were old friends. He felt the need to cheer her up, so he kept her laughing for the entire ride.

"So where do I go now?" he asked.

"Turn right, then right again. The funeral home is really behind the church."

Juan thought back to the deliveries he had made here. He'd known there was a funeral home around here somewhere, had to be. Who knew he would be running around with the funeral home heiress herself?

"Don't you have to go to funeral home school or something if you want to run a funeral home?" They were pulling into the parking lot. The sign indicating Chappee Funeral Home was simple, but it ran the entire length of the building.

"My grandfather did. He went to mortuary school. He wanted me to go, too, but he wanted me to go to traditional college first. You know, learn business stuff. A mortician can be hired. I went for two semesters and then my grandmother died. Then last year I started taking just music classes."

Juan turned off the ignition and handed Angelica her keys. He wanted to say he was sorry, but somehow knew that Angelica would not appreciate it. She seemed so strong for someone with so much recent tragedy in her life.

Angelica opened her car door, searching for the key to the funeral home. She found the key and turned, noticing that Juan was still sitting in the car. She smiled and motioned for him to follow.

He admired the view from behind as he followed Angelica, glancing over at the church, now behind them. It looked just as big and modern as it did from the front, in direct contrast to the simple but large funeral home building. He realized the only thing that really was between the church and here was more parking. These two were the only buildings on the equivalent of a city block.

Juan shuddered. In his mind he saw people going in the

front of Lost Pilgrim and getting wheeled out the back door, right into the funeral home. Constant business. Angelica's grandfather was certainly a shrewd businessman. He closed the car door and followed her into the building.

The inside of the funeral home was not too different from that of a church. It was pitch-black. Angelica went into the darkness to turn on the lights. In the back where he stood, he could make out a small table with papers on it, with a glass wall in front that led to the service area, which also served as a viewing room.

Lights began to flood the building, and Angelica returned, looking nervous again. "My grandfather's office is down front, to the left of the lectern. I'm going to go in there for a while. You are welcome to come if you like."

Juan shook his head. "I think you should have some private time alone. Have you been here since he died?"

Tears sprang to Angelica's eyes. She sniffed them back, shaking her head. "No, not since his funeral."

"You go. I'll find me a seat."

He watched as Angelica disappeared through a small door to the right. Juan looked around, able to see clearly now. The table he spotted when they had entered was decorated with an arrangement of flowers, now drying. He touched them, and some leaves came off and fluttered to the table, landing on top of a funeral program.

Juan picked it up and turned it over. It was from Angelica's grandfather's funeral service. He read the biography on the back. The only remaining relative mentioned was Angelica. It was sad. Angelica's grandmother was also mentioned as having died not too long ago. They were apparently married a long time, since her grandmother was sixteen. Angelica had not told him that. He read further. The Chappee family owned several funeral homes. Angelica was about to be very loaded.

Juan returned the program to where he found it and swept the droppings from the flowers together with his hand. He stepped inside the viewing area, taking a seat in the back. Juan was prepared to wait.

30

Ché wet her lips. She couldn't see who it was that was actually driving the car, but it didn't matter. It looked like Angelica was on her way to the funeral home instead of over to the church. She looked at her watch. Strange, for this time of night. Her mother drove up and blinked the headlights. Ché remained paralyzed. Maybe Angelica needed to go there first for something, perhaps a checkbook. Maybe she was going to give money to the church after all.

Deborah rolled down the window and yelled at Ché.

"You getting in or what? I got to go on home, there's a lot I have to do tonight." She was back to her old self. The few minutes alone in the car seemed to be enough for Deborah to get herself together.

Ché was almost relieved at the familiar grating sound of her mother's voice. She glanced at the corner where she last saw Angelica's car again.

"Ma, I need to talk to the pastor a minute." She bounced up and down, impatient.

"You need to go to the bathroom? You want me to wait or you want to ride with him?" she said. "You know he can stay here real late."

She nodded at her mother and didn't answer. She would get home. Deborah opened her mouth to speak, and Ché took off and headed back into the church building.

She ran across the church lobby and down the hall, skidding as she made the corner. She headed toward the back of the building, past the voices she heard coming from the choir room. She reached a door marked EXIT, the glowing sign the only dim light in this part of the build-ing. Using her whole body weight, she pushed the door open, kicking the door stop wedge to keep the door slightly ajar.

There were no cars in the rear parking lot. Ché looked across to the funeral home and saw Angelica's car parked in front. Lights were on inside the building. Bingo.

She jogged across the parking lot. Maybe Angelica would see she meant business now. She didn't want to go home and deal with her mother, not the way she was acting lately. She pulled the heavy door open and stepped inside. It shut behind her with a thud. She jumped at the sound. An empty funeral home was still a funeral home. She shivered as she felt her skin crawl.

The vestibule was lit, but half the building, the right side, was in semidarkness. She did not see Angelica, but she noticed a small light at the front, coming from what Ché knew was the office.

She hurried down the left side of the building and disappeared into the room.

31

Angelica fondly ran her fingers over the top of her grandfather's desk. He was such an enigma: He loved technology but could not bear to part with this old-fashioned rolltop desk. She remembered him restoring it in the garage at their house. He worked on the desk for days. Then he motorized the rolltop. It was an anachronism all by itself.

Angelica picked up the remote and pushed a button. The top of the desk opened, emitting a very high-tech swoosh. It still worked like a charm. She smiled, walked around the desk, and sat in her grandfather's chair.

The chair swiveled freely, and Angelica wondered why she had not taken some time before this just to think. It made so much sense. Had her grandfather envisioned all this? Angelica turned the chair around and stared out the window. She found herself in an almost trancelike state, toying with the remote in her hands.

She felt the air change in the building, and she knew the

front door had been opened. Juan had probably stepped out-side. She smiled, thinking about him. She had only known him a short time and he had already helped her so much.

Suddenly Ché was standing at the front of the desk.

"So," Ché said. "Did you forget something tonight?" She stood with her arms crossed, tapping her left foot on the floor.

Angelica jumped. She looked past Ché for Juan. This was too much for her right now.

"Didn't I make myself clear?" Ché walked around to the side of the desk as she spoke. She didn't wait for Angelica to an-swer. "Donation, remember? Trustee meeting? You missed it."

Angelica knew exactly what she was talking about and didn't want to be reminded. She stood up. "Look, I am tired of this. I don't care what you tell anyone. You just do what you think is right." She placed her forehead in her hand and rubbed. A headache was coming.

"Well, I don't think you mean that. You don't want your family name dragged through the mud, do you? There have been new 'developments.'" Ché made quote signs in the air with her fingers. "Didn't you get my message?"

Angelica raised her eyebrows. She could feel the anger welling up inside her. "Oh?" she said. "How about this for a new 'development.' " Angelica mimicked Ché, making quote signs of her own. "I don't care. I am not giving the church a thing. You don't even know if my grandfather left me anything at all. You people didn't even give me a chance to begin grieving for him. You obviously don't give a damn about him, me, or our family."

32

The semidarkness was good for Juan. He sat patiently as it enveloped him, his mind calm. He did not think about how much he hated the dry-cleaning business, or even about how much he loved his music. Not this time. He didn't even think about his performance at the end of the week. He'd already played his best when he played to Angelica. He just sat, feeling hugged by the room, and almost drifted off to sleep.

Juan enjoyed the calmness he was feeling since he'd met Angelica. They'd shared so much, mainly about her. It was almost as if she were waiting for him to happen, to let a whole load roll off her shoulders. That wasn't a bad thing, Juan didn't mind, but he had not shared much about himself. He had not told Angelica about his situation, that his father wanted him to take over the family business and he didn't want to. But he noticed Angelica was trying to find a way to solve her problems, and the only solution he thought about for his was running.

All the talk about following your heart was the same stuff that James had been telling Juan for years, and Juan had blown him off. Sometimes during those discussions, Juan felt like James just wanted him out of the way. Now when Juan listened to himself telling Angelica the very same things that James told him, it made a lot more sense to him. James just had his best interests in mind all along. Juan suddenly felt guilty for the resentment he was feeling lately toward James. Perhaps if he had told his father the truth and insisted that he listen back when he'd first started feeling that he wanted to do something else, it wouldn't be so difficult now. He knew one thing for sure, he wanted to talk to his father while he still could. Maybe they could work out some compromise. That was sure better than waiting until he was dead to talk to his glass of water or making some confession at his grave. He would bring it up in their call tonight, after his father was reassured that all of the day's business was taken care of.

After ten minutes of waiting, his cell phone vibrated in his pocket. In the coziness of his near-sleep, the movement startled him. He removed the phone from his pocket and stared at it as if it were something he had never seen before. In fact, he'd forgotten that it was in his pocket at all.

The light from the dim screen seemed bright in the near-darkness of the funeral home. The infinity symbol seemed to scream at him; he had a new voice message. He knew who it was and what it said. Juan had not touched base with James and the plant for what seemed like hours, even though he knew the deliveries were backing up. He knew the work still needed to get done, no matter how long it took. With Angelica, he'd put all business out of his mind.

He dialed his voice mail. Just as he thought, James's voice bellowed at him.

"Juan," James's message yelled, "where the hell are you? I need your input on something. We have some broken machinery. I'm going to hunt down a spare part. Can you meet me over at the plant ASAP?"

It was time for him to check in on Angelica anyway. He smoothed his clothing and started to get up. At that moment, Juan heard the front door of the building open and then slam shut. He looked up, immediately on guard, intending to see who entered the building. According to Angelica, her grandfather was well known, so most people would know that the funeral home was closed right now.

Before he could get up and head toward the door, Juan saw a woman run down the aisle so fast that she didn't even hear him call out to her. She made a beeline straight for the office where Angelica was.

Juan paused. She obviously knew where to go. Perhaps she had seen Angelica's car outside. He stood up to stretch. She must be a friend of Angelica's.

The phone vibrated again and it was less surprising this time. He knew James needed him back at the plant. Although it was against his better judgment, Juan did not answer the phone. If James found out where he was, he would never live it down, and he just didn't feel up to the teasing.

Juan turned the phone off and headed down the aisle to

the office. As he got closer, he could hear Angelica talking to the person who had just entered. Her voice sounded loud and agitated.

Juan paused outside the door to the office a minute. Although he had not recognized the woman when she ran by, her voice when she replied had a familiar quality to it, but he couldn't quite place it. Since he'd talked with so many new people this week, that didn't surprise him. What was a surprise was how upset Angelica sounded. He stepped into the doorway.

"Everything all right, ladies?"

Angelica looked up from where she was sitting. Relief flooded her face.

"Oh, I wasn't aware there was anyone else here with you, Angelica," Ché said.

"I tried to talk to you when you came in. I was sitting over on the other side of the funeral home. I'm Juan." He extended his hand toward Ché.

She didn't take it. "I'm sorry. Are you Angelica's new boyfriend? I don't think we have met."

"We haven't. I am with Spotless Cleaners, by Delgado. Just in town to service the choir convention and competition. Is there a problem here, Angelica?"

Ché did not let Angelica answer. "No, there isn't. Not yet." She touched her chin. "My stepfather mentioned you. Your father bought that old dry-cleaning place downtown."

"That's right." He nodded and looked over at Angelica for a cue as to how he should proceed. "Angelica, are you about ready? They've been calling me at the plant; I need to go over and check in."

"Actually," Ché said, "we were having a discussion—"

"A discussion that is over. I'm ready, Juan." Angelica stood up, the remote still in her hand.

Ché felt panic begin in her stomach. "I don't care if he knows your business if you don't. I don't think we are finished here." Her voice quavered. She put her hand on her hips, slinging her braids to the side.

"There's nothing to tell, Ché. The church will get whatever it is my grandfather wanted. From what I can tell, that is nothing. Would you mind leaving so I can lock up?"

Ché was stunned, but she drew herself up and turned to leave. Juan looked from Ché to Angelica, and it suddenly hit him. He had heard her voice at Mt. Moriah, while he was in the bathroom. This was the voice he'd heard about through the vent. And this was the Angelica she was talking about!

The day when he picked up the bin of robes from Mt. Moriah, the two women he heard sounded venomous enough that he wanted to turn and run, and he had. But from the looks of things, Angelica seemed to be handling this quite well. The person before him didn't seem so threatening now. Instead, he almost pitied Ché, mostly because she seemed so desperate. Juan remembered the threats the other woman had made. He stepped out of the way so that Ché could get by.

"Thanks for waiting for me." Angelica closed all the blinds in the room, returning the office to the way she'd found it. "This was a good idea. It helped me to clear my head." She took Juan's hand.

He smiled. "No problem. You wanna fill me in?"

Angelica shrugged. "You mean about what I decided . . . or about that?" She motioned toward the door, referring to Ché.

"Let's start with her. Do I need to watch my back or what? I can't believe I've been here less than a week and have managed to get caught up in some soap-opera-sounding crap." He grinned and held her hand tighter.

"Well, how about you fill me in on all this dry-cleaning stuff that Ché was talking about? How do you know Ché's father? I thought you were a musician." Angelica realized she had been talking nonstop about herself.

He glanced at his watch. "I guess you're going to have to come with me. We can talk about it on the way."

"How is it possible to feel like you know a person so well and then not know them at all?" Angelica winked. "I've been so busy talking about myself that I haven't asked anything about you, have I?" She blushed as they walked to the door.

"That's okay. Maybe I wasn't ready to tell yet. I have got some talking to do to more than one person."

They were silent for a minute. Juan stood by the passenger side of the car as Angelica locked the door to the funeral home. She turned around and smiled, throwing the keys in his direction. He flashed a mischievous grin as he caught them. He was going to be in both the driving and the talking seat for a while.

33

Ché stepped out of the funeral home. The air was colder than she remembered. She could not believe that Angelica just decided that she was not going to give anything to the church. She had to find a way to tell her mother; Deborah said she was counting on using that money to divert attention away from the financial problems of the church.

She hurried back across the parking lot, trying to formulate the correct words in her mind. She also tried to imagine the correct distance to stand away from Deborah in case she went postal again and started swinging.

On a night when everything else had gone wrong, she was grateful that the door she'd wedged open in the church was still ajar. She pushed it open and stepped into the building, then glanced at her watch. She'd been gone about fifteen minutes. Her mother was probably furious at the way Ché had left her. She broke into a jog as she attempted to get past her stepfather's office. Just as she did, she heard her mother's voice.

"Ché, have you lost you mind, girl?"

Ché cringed. Her mother's icy voice grabbed hold of her, stopping her short in her tracks. She turned around to see her mother step out of her stepfather's office.

"Well, where have you been? I thought you had to go to the bathroom or something. You knew I was waiting for you, right?"

Ché didn't answer, but the look on her face probably betrayed her feelings. Deborah strode closer, grabbing Ché on the shoulder.

"Well?" she demanded, shaking her as if doing so would cause words to drop out of her mouth.

"Ma, people will see you." Ché could only manage a squeak.

"I don't care. What is going on? Spill it!" Deborah's voice was rising with each word. Ché recognized the familiar irrational look clouding her mother's face.

"Okay, I went to the funeral home. Angelica was there." Ché's words ran out of her like they were her lifeline. She was vaguely aware of pain where Deborah's perfectly manicured nails were digging into her shoulder. "I have been blackmailing her, sort of, to get her to give money to the church." Ché cowered, expecting her mother to hit her again.

Deborah was silent, releasing her grip. Ché fell backward, almost losing her balance. Deborah grabbed her again, more gently this time, and stepped closer, pushing Ché to the middle of the hallway.

"Did I tell you to do that?" Ché could hear the venom in her voice. "Did I?"

"No, Ma." She looked at the ground. "I just thought it would be better. I just wanted to make you happy." Tears welled in her eyes.

"You haven't been able to make me happy since that unfortunate incident with my foster brother brought you here. But that has been my cross to bear, now, hasn't it?"

Ché felt herself stop breathing. Her mother's words pierced her heart like a stake. She wasn't stupid. She knew her mother hated her. Deborah told her repeatedly all the things that she would have done had it not been for Ché being born. She dried her tears with her sleeve. She didn't know why she thought she could change that or make her mother resent her less.

Deborah continued. "All I wanted you to do was make friends with her. That's all. What happened?"

"I saw her in the hotel that first day. At the conference." Ché kept her eyes on the floor as she spoke. "She was with a guy and—"

"And you thought you would use that to your advantage, right? Maybe get a little something for yourself, too? Is that what you thought? Have you turned against me, too?"

Ché didn't answer. At this point, her mother would believe whatever she wanted to anyway.

Deborah was trembling with anger. "I'm talking to you! Don't ignore me." She grabbed Ché's face, pressing her chin between her fingers. "Where is she now? I will just go reason with her myself! I should have done that in the first place."

"She left with the dry-cleaning guy. Juan. He took her to the Spotless Cleaners, I think." Tears welled up in Ché's eyes again. She fought them back. Her mother still had only one thing on her mind. She didn't care about Ché.

"Fine." Deborah let her daughter go, composing herself again. "I'll just meet them there. Hopefully you haven't ruined everything."

Ché watched as her mother took out her compact and reapplied her makeup although she didn't need it.

Deborah did not say another word as she clicked away, down the hall of Mt. Moriah. She did not look back as she walked out to her car and prepared to leave. She knew exactly where the dry-cleaning plant was downtown. She put the car in gear, and before taking her foot off the brake, she quickly unzipped her bag and checked her "insurance," the .22 revolver that her husband usually kept in his desk.

34

Bill Davis stepped into the hallway outside his office. He had just returned there from the meeting that was still going on in the sanctuary. Ché was standing there, tears streaming down her face.

"What's going on?" he said.

Ché sniffled, but did not speak at first. He looked up and down the hallway as he strode over to her.

"Your mother upset about the trustee meeting? She didn't have nice things to say to me about it, either. It certainly isn't your fault. I don't know what has gotten into her." He shook his head. "She really seems to be taking this trustee business to heart."

"That and everything else." Ché could barely get the words out of her mouth. She was tired of her mother and her whole tirade.

Bill put his hand on her shoulder. "What do you mean?"

"She blames me for everything. It's all my fault. She says

that I stopped her from living her life." Ché was now sobbing uncontrollably.

Bill embraced Ché, attempting to comfort her. He looked up and down the hallway again, surprised that no one else seemed to have seen her crying or heard the ruckus. He guided her into his office and closed the door.

Ché carefully sat down on the leather furniture. She couldn't recall ever being in the office with him alone since she and her mother had arrived in town. The pastor leaned back on his desk in front of her.

"Okay, just calm down, now. Tell me what you're talking about." He was supposed to counsel the members of his congregation; he should be able to talk to his own stepdaughter. He knew so little about her, and really, so little about her mother, too.

Ché paused for a minute. Her mother would kill her if she told this man their business. But the way she was acting lately, she would kill her anyway. Things were just getting far too crazy, stranger than they had ever been.

"My mother hates me. She blames me for all of her troubles. But I did mess up this time. I thought I was helping." Ché wiped her tears on her sleeve again. Bill reached over and handed her the box of tissues that were sitting on his credenza.

"She's always told me that her last foster mother was good to her and she could have been anything if it weren't for me. She blames it on me that the woman kicked her out. No one would have known that her foster brother practically raped her if I hadn't been born. But I was, and she blames me for everything."

Bill watched as Ché sobbed, not knowing whether he should try to comfort her or not. He was amazed at this mystery from his wife's past. Deborah had never discussed this with him. He had not known the circumstances around Ché's birth before. Deborah told him that she'd loved Ché's father.

"And she's mad about that now? That was a long time ago . . . and she should have been happy that she got out of an unhealthy situation."

"At this moment, she's mad because I messed up her plan to get money from Angelica Chappee. She wanted me to be friendly with her and . . ."

"You refused to be part of her plan?"

"No, I actually sort of made my own plan. I tried to blackmail Angelica instead and it backfired. Both of them hate me now." Ché started to sob again.

Bill paused. "I told her to leave that girl alone when she mentioned her crazy idea. The church will work out its own problems." He stood up from his desk and walked across the office. "Would you mind filling me in on why she is so hard-headed?"

"Mama thinks she's entitled to the money. She said that Chappee owes it to her. She told me that a lot of stuff that happened to her family was his fault." Ché threw her disintegrating tissue into the trash and reached for a new one. "I just wanted someone else to be blamed for something for a change. It didn't make sense to me, but I didn't care."

"Happened to her family? Like what?" Bill said.

Ché shrugged. "She was talking crazy, now that I think

about it. It didn't make sense. She said that her mother killed herself because of him or something. I didn't understand her and she said she would tell me the whole story later. She has old newspaper clippings of him, from when he was young. And some kind of diary I think must have been my grandmother's. In that box she keeps. I couldn't see all of it."

"I knew her mother killed herself, but not because she told me. Ben told me, when you first came here. That is what we fought about. There's a lot we both don't know, Ché. Your mother's family was really screwed up. I would never have known what I do if it weren't for Ben. But I didn't care, I thought that I could change her. I wanted to help." He rubbed his temples.

"Change her? You knew?"

"Oh, I knew all about your mother's marrying past. Ben Chappee made sure I did. I accused him of meddling. We had been friends a long time, but I stopped talking to him because of all this. I told him he just didn't want me to be happy." Bill's eyes were wide as he searched his stepdaughter's face. "How much do you know about your mother's family?" he asked.

"Her real family? Almost nothing. I don't even know that much about her last foster family. She doesn't talk about them much."

Pastor Davis stood up suddenly, a look of urgency in his face. "I guess she wouldn't tell you everything. She would probably be ashamed of them. She was upset when she left just now, right? Where did she go?"

He put on his jacket. His sudden decisiveness surprised Ché.

"She went to the Spotless Cleaners, I think. That's where she thinks Angelica is going. Why?"

"We should meet her there. She sounds irrational. Let's go."

Ché followed his lead, marveling at the sudden backbone her stepfather was showing. She remembered her mother complaining about his lack of ability to stand up for himself, but he seemed to be determined to intercept Deborah, determined to find out what was going on. Ché found a new respect for him. She just hoped he could deal with it once they confronted her mother.

35

"So you heard someone talking, two people, through the vents at the church?" Angelica pressed her fingers to her forehead where her headache was.

"Yes, she sounded just like Ché, too, and she was talking to another woman. I think she called her 'Ma.' "

"That would have been the pastor's wife, Deborah. And how do you know they were talking about me?" Angelica could not believe that Juan had overheard Ché planning to blackmail her. This town suddenly seemed too small.

They were sitting at a light on the way to the Delgado Brothers' plant.

"Well, she mentioned the name Angelica, which at the time meant nothing to me." Juan smiled at her. He wanted to calm her nerves.

"I told her I am not giving them anything, and I mean it. As a matter of fact, I may not get anything to give anyway."

"So I guess that means—"

"No guessing. You have no idea how crazy the whole thing is getting. I've spent several days doing all kinds of crazy things to try and lose my virginity. My grandfather must be turning over in his grave. I can't believe he wanted me to do that. I don't think he did." She folded her arms and looked out the window.

While sitting in her grandfather's office, Angelica thought long and hard. By the time Ché had shown up, she knew in her heart what she should do.

Obviously, the crazy requirement her Pop-pop had invented for her to come into her inheritance was not right for her. Either her grandfather wanted her to discover this or he really was not in his right mind when he recorded his will. The best she could do was to go with her gut feeling.

"One thing is for sure," Juan said. "I don't think you've heard the last of Ché. The other woman I heard in the bathroom was pushing her to get to you. And she sounded serious. So serious that I don't think a simple no would put her off. She sounded like she was counting on that money."

Angelica nodded. Juan was right, she couldn't be too careful. Especially if they thought she was worth millions of dollars.

"I bet they're connected to the money shortage at the church somehow. Why else would she be so desperate? I never trusted either of them."

Juan pulled the car into the alley behind the dry-cleaning plant.

"Sorry you have to see this from the back like this. But

coming in from the front wouldn't make it any prettier," he said. His voice softened. "Welcome to my family business. This is *my* inheritance."

Juan parked and Angelica stepped out hesitantly. She glanced over the debris-littered alley, then at the building. It was wedged in between the other, similar buildings. The main difference was the smell of dry-cleaning chemicals from Juan's building and the sign; it had a light out on the letter *L*.

"It ain't much, but the plant back home in the Bronx is much bigger."

"Your father must be very proud. Everything is all figured out for you. You are so lucky. I wish it was that simple for me. You know, my grandfather's lawyer's office is right over there." Angelica pointed in the direction of Lieberman's office. "You and I have been moving around in the same areas all week and didn't even know it." Angelica felt tears spring to her eyes as she remembered viewing her grandfather's will. "Your father must have a lot of faith in you to send you down here like he did."

"Yeah, he does." Juan paused for a second. He suddenly felt like an idiot. "But I think he will understand me better if I sit down and talk with him instead of yell for a change," he said.

"You mean you're going to follow the advice you've been giving me?" Angelica smiled.

Juan didn't answer. Instead they began walking up the alley toward the office door. He fished in his pocket for his key, but instead pulled out an unused packet of raw sugar.

He banged on the metal door with the side of his fist and rang the bell simultaneously.

Angelica raised one eyebrow, looking up at Juan from the corner of her eye.

"I thought most dry-cleaning wizards carried their keys with them," she said.

"You don't know me well enough to tease me yet." But Juan laughed, then began banging on the door again. "There should be someone here. The machines are loud inside. We should only have to wait a minute."

"Angelica Chappee."

Angelica and Juan spun around to face Deborah standing behind them. There was a half smile on her pinched face, and her arms were crossed.

"Got a new boyfriend, huh? Are you sure he doesn't want you just for your money? Everyone wants something and I know you have heard that men are good for nothing. I would be careful if I were you. And didn't your grandfather teach you better than to go into alleyways with men like this?" Deborah moved a step closer and her lips curled into a heinous grin that bared her teeth.

Angelica was shocked. She had not expected to hear from Deborah or her daughter again so quickly. She stuttered, frozen in place. "Did you f-f-follow us here? How did you—"

"Ché told me, like a good little girl. You know, you gave my baby quite a fright. Now, what is this I hear about you not giving any money to your church?" Deborah emphasized the *your,* as if trying to drive a point home to Angelica.

Juan could see the deranged look in Deborah's eyes. It was one that he recognized. He remembered that look in the eyes of homeless people on Bronx streets. She was desperate, but far more so than the way she sounded that day through the vent in the church bathroom.

"Why don't you just leave her alone?" he said. He stepped in front of Angelica.

Deborah's hands dropped down to her side and revealed the handgun she had been concealing "Look, *lover boy*. This is local business. It has nothing to do with you. Miss Thing here owes it to her church. She owes it to me. It's none of your business."

Deborah flinched, using her free hand to swat at the air above her head as if gnats were buzzing around her head.

Both Angelica and Juan were silent. They'd had no idea how crazy Deborah really was. The gun in her hand confirmed it. No wonder Ché had been so persistent.

"Did you have any idea that we go way back, Angelica? Did you? Well, let me tell you how far. I came here to get to know my father. I grew up without him, or my mother, in foster care. But you wouldn't know any of that, would you?" Deborah twitched, swatting at the air again.

"You see, my mother, Denise, had a lover when she was about fifteen years old. He was an older man, and she got pregnant the first time they were ever together. She never told anyone his name, and she had the baby, me, all alone, in a hospital. Then they drugged her and took her baby away from her. That was about thirty-five years ago, when you could still commit people. Then the man married someone else, without even seeing me or asking about me. My mother was heartbroken. She killed herself because of it. Promptly jumped out of a window, right in the hospital." Deborah paused, searching the faces of Angelica and Juan for a reaction. "I never got to know her.

"I know you think I'm crazy, but the story's not finished." She pointed the gun at Angelica. "She left me a note, one that no one ever paid attention to, not since they knew that my mother was crazy. Make that *had* been. She was dead, remember? I grew up in foster homes. My mother's relatives couldn't live with the truth. They didn't want me, but they didn't want to let me go, either. When I was eighteen, they gave me the note my mother had written, along with some of her personal things. Finally I was allowed to know who my father was. I have carried it with me ever since. I knew I would find him one day." Deborah licked her lips. She removed one of her hands from the gun she was pointing at them and smoothed her hair.

Angelica's eyes went from Deborah's face to her trembling hands. "What does that have to do with me?" Angelica's voice quavered. Juan put his hand on her arm.

"You are really a nimwit. You don't deserve all that money. Don't you get it yet? My father was your grandfather. Bill Chappee. Call me Auntie." Deborah's face hardened. Angelica gasped, almost losing her balance. Juan steadied her.

"I can't believe that my grandfather would just ignore his child. I know you're making this up because that doesn't even sound like him. He was so—"

"Responsible? Yeah, right." Deborah took a step toward Juan and Angelica. She put her finger on the trigger of the gun. "Age will do that to people. He didn't care about my mother, not really. She was young and vulnerable and she trusted him. To him, she was just a young piece of ass. Otherwise he would have taken care of his responsibilities. He didn't even look back."

Angelica thought about her grandfather. For someone so virtuous, he sure did know a lot about the world. She remembered him telling her about his escapades in his younger days. Maybe he had cleaned them up a little for her. Maybe some of Deborah's story was true. How could anyone just make up a story like this?

"So you see, I am really being nice to you in asking you to give money to the church. It's the easy way, really." Deborah swatted at the air again. As she did, she waved the gun around, pointing it in all directions. Juan and Angelica ducked a little, trying to avoid her aim.

"Did I say move?" Deborah steadied herself once again and put both hands back on the gun. "I could make it harder for you and contest the will to get what is rightfully mine. This thing could drag on a long time. We would have to dig up old hospital records. A donation would be the best thing." She began to walk closer to Angelica and Juan. They backed away, toward the building. At the same instant, a figure jumped from the shadows, knocking Deborah to the ground. It was James. He twisted Deborah's wrist, freeing the gun from her hand as she screamed at the top of her lungs. She tried to fight, but James was too much for her. He overpowered her and pinned her to the ground.

Both Juan and Angelica watched, stunned.

"All I wanted was to get to know him. To have him acknowledge me, admit that he did love my mother. I know some loves are forbidden, I could have forgiven him for that. But he died too fast. Before I could—" Deborah's screams gave way to sobbing. James let her go and she rolled over in the alley, continuing to cry, defeated.

"I had no idea she was really this crazy," Angelica said, covering her face with her hands. Her headache throbbed.

Ché and Pastor Davis were now standing behind James. Ché immediately knelt at her mother's side.

"The police should be on the way," Pastor Davis said. "We listened to the whole thing. Angelica, I am really sorry for all this trouble. I should have realized what was going on sooner. Ben Chappee said she wanted something. I would have never guessed it would come to this."

Angelica looked around in disbelief at the people in the now-crowded alley. Juan put his arm around her again, leading Angelica inside the building. He and James made eye contact and James shrugged his shoulders. This was nuttier than he'd ever imagined.

Inside the dry-cleaning plant, Juan led Angelica to a seat behind the usually vacant desk. James brought her a glass of water. She was shaking visibly, although the plant was very warm from the heat of the dry-cleaning machines.

"That was some scene, huh, Jefe?" James said.

Juan looked from James to Angelica. "Yeah, it was." He

was hoping that James wouldn't talk too much for a change. His stomach was still churning from the possibility that Deborah could have used that gun.

"Good thing I had your back, you know?" James was looking more for confirmation than for thanks. He still was not too sure what had transpired in the alley.

"Good thing. But you always do." Juan signaled with his eyes for his friend to be silent. Deborah's words would be shocking to anybody, and he was sure that Angelica was confused. He certainly was.

36

Ché was stupefied as she watched the ambulance take her mother away. She and Pastor Davis had listened from the sidelines as Deborah told her twisted story to Angelica. They were spellbound until she pulled the gun.

Thank goodness for James. Ché had not met him before, but she was thankful he had intercepted her mother before she could do serious damage to Angelica or to herself.

She now understood why her mother felt she was entitled to Angelica's money. She thought she was actually Angelica's aunt. That made a lot of things clearer. But Ché did not understand her mother's irrational approach. Why had she begun acting so crazy?

Bill was shocked himself. He didn't realize that Deborah knew he kept a gun at the church, and he could have kicked himself for not making sure it was locked up. He was going to have more explaining to do about that later. He tapped

Ché on the shoulder after the ambulance left, guiding her to the car.

"That stuff your mother was talking about, it's not all true, you know," he said.

"So are you saying my mother is crazier than it looks?" Ché shook her head in disbelief. It couldn't get any worse than it was.

"She has some things to sort out, but she is misguided, too. Chappee is not her father. I know that for a fact."

He held the door for Ché. He wondered how much she had known about her mother. He couldn't believe it took him this long to realize that something was seriously wrong. Ben Chappee had tried to tell him, but he wouldn't listen.

"How do you know that? She said her mother left her a note."

"I don't doubt that she did. But I grew up with Ben Chappee. He was never associated with Deborah's mother. He did have a shotgun wedding, but that was to the love of his life. He married Angelica's grandmother when she was very young and pregnant. He moved to Baton Rouge not too long after. He was my best friend, and I followed him."

"So why didn't my mother know that? She asked you questions about him, but you never gave her answers."

"Ben and I had a falling out. He was mad at me when I told him about your mother and the ad I had on the Internet. He thought that was too ridiculous. He had his fancy private investigators check her out before you two moved here."

Ché was aghast. Then they knew about her past all along. They must have. "So you knew about—"

"Yes, we knew that she had married several times before, and that they were all preachers. We knew that all of the marriages ended abruptly. We even knew that all of the churches had financial issues. But she was never implicated. But I didn't find out that she was Denise's daughter until much later. I definitely didn't know about the letter." Bill wiped his brow with the back of his sleeve. "I should have put the whole thing together."

"Denise came to live in our town with one of our neighbors. We called her Ma'dear, everyone did. Ma'dear was such a sweet old lady. Denise was sent to live with Ma'dear—Denise was her cousin or something. Denise's parents were supposed to follow her later. Folks used to do that type of thing all the time back then. They would want to move north, for a better life, but they couldn't afford for everyone to go at the same time. Anyway, the family was never reunited. It was a big scandal."

"What was so scandalous about that?" Ché asked.

"Denise kind of kept to herself. Lots of the kids in the neighborhood teased her, said she was different. She used to talk to herself all the time, and didn't make friends very easily. She got pregnant, and then disappeared. She jumped out of a hospital window. It was in all the newspapers.

"We found out later that she was being molested by the man of the house, Ma'dear's husband. Our neighborhood was devastated. The family had been a pillar of the community for years. Ma'dear moved away when they took her husband away to jail. They say she was never the same."

"So why would my mother think that Ben Chappee was her father?"

"That part I don't know. He was quite the ladies' man, though. All the young girls had a crush on him. Maybe she did, too."

"The diary. It must have been Denise's. She mentions being with a man she identifies as just B. But she also talks about hearing voices."

"That could be. Sometimes people hallucinate, especially in painful situations. Maybe she only imagined that Ben was her lover. Ben was quite the charmer. He was so nice to everyone."

Ché wiped her hand over her face. "But we'll never know now, not for sure."

Bill put his hand on her shoulder, shaking his head. "No, we won't. And sometimes unstableness like that runs in families. It may have been outside her control. No wonder Deb is the way she is. And you know, years ago, Ben started receiving mysterious phone calls. I think he even got a letter from someone claiming to be his child. Nothing ever came of it. We thought it might have been a misguided prank. It was around the same time Angelica was born, though. That was a scandal in itself because his own daughter was so young then."

"So I guess the answers died with my grandmother, huh?"

He looked over at Ché, realizing the effect this news must

be having on her. "You have a home here. You know that, right?"

Ché was confused. She wasn't sure about anything anymore. Her mother had more secrets than she had realized. Ché was finally beginning to understand her mother's statements about blaming Ben Chappee for everything that had happened to her. She really did think he was responsible. Deborah falsely believed her mother had killed herself because he'd left her. The thought that Ben Chappee might be her grandfather had kind of excited her at first, because she'd thought finally she knew a little something about her family. The family her mother never talked about. But that was a lie, too.

"But child welfare will probably take me away from you," she replied. "I have over a year before I turn eighteen. And Mama said that you two weren't even married."

Bill shook his head. "I don't think they will. There will probably be an investigation, though. And it is true that your mother wasn't married to the last guy. I checked. But her first husband died two weeks before our wedding. That makes us legal. I plan to stick by her, and that means taking care of you, if you want to stay."

Ché didn't know what she wanted to do. Everything was all confused. She shrugged and stared out the window. Her stepfather had been good to her up to now. She sighed. All of this because one woman, years dead, had had a secret crush on someone who probably hadn't even given her the time of day. Men caused so much trouble. She didn't want to think about it right now.

37

The offices of Lieberman and Associates did not seem as intimidating to Angelica now as they had a week ago. They still appeared lavish—the leather was still spotless and the lithographs still tasteful. But now Angelica felt more in control and less uncertain of her future. Jeanette was with her again, and she was glad she wasn't alone. Her friend had been the one constant through this ordeal, even though Angelica hadn't filled her in on all the details until it was all over.

The receptionist was working today, unlike last week, and she barely looked up from the tedious job of filing her nails. She answered the constantly ringing phones the same way, as if Angelica and those calling were secondary to the task of completing her manicure. When Angelica walked in, she held up one clawed finger and summoned Lieberman without so much as a hello. Jeanette rolled her eyes and then sat on the sofa without being asked.

Angelica sat as well, fingering the magazines on the glass table. She'd asked Juan to come with her, too, but he declined her offer; he had to tie up loose ends at the dry-cleaning plant, and told her that she probably ought to do this on her own anyway. It was just as well; Angelica realized that she was going to have to learn to find strength from within. Her Pop-pop was gone and she needed to get used to being on her own.

The past week had been a rude awakening. Angelica was shaken, but the truth was now in the open. She felt sorry for Deborah a little. The poor woman had lived her entire life believing a lie. Angelica loved her grandfather dearly, and although it turned out that he was not Deborah's father, she realized that he probably had been no saint in his life. But that was in the past now.

At least she understood his feelings toward Lost Pilgrim a little better. She'd had no idea that Pastor Davis had grown up with her grandfather. It was silly how lifelong friends let things come between them like they did.

Lieberman finally strode into the room, looking as unfriendly as he did that day at the cemetery. Angelica stood up to meet him, wondering briefly how he had met her grandfather. She would probably never know. They shook hands, and he motioned for her to follow. Jeanette had her head buried in a *People* magazine and didn't attempt to follow. They walked back to the same conference room Angelica had sat in the week before.

Lieberman closed the door behind Angelica and walked around to the other side of the table again. He leaned on the long table, each hand resting on top of a videotape.

"Well," he said. His face showed no sign of emotion, making it hard for Angelica to read him. "Did you lose your virginity?"

Angelica drew herself up, gathering her courage. She wanted to sound confident. "I can't believe that my grandfather asked me to do what I saw him ask me to do on that tape." She folded her hands in front of her. "Quite honestly, Mr. Lieberman, I spent a lot of time looking silly and agonizing over what to do. Finally, I thought about it and decided that I was just not ready, and no amount of money could bring me to give up what I believe in. Now, I loved my Pop-pop, but in the end I just had to go with my gut feeling. The time was just not right. So, to make a long story short"— Angelica took a deep breath—"I don't have a doctor's note for you."

Leiberman leaned back. Angelica watched his face, and for the first time since she'd met the man, he smiled.

"Well, then. Your grandfather left two tapes, one just for this occasion."

Lieberman took the tape under his right hand and turned, placing it in the VCR. Angelica waited, holding her breath. Her grandfather appeared on the screen, in the same place he had been in the original tape.

"Well, hello, baby girl." He smiled at her just as he had last time. Angelica felt her eyes moisten. "It's hard to believe I have been dead more than a week, huh?"

Angelica felt herself smile. "If you are watching this tape, it means you didn't do what I asked you to in the first half of the other one." He paused, taking a drink from a small glass of water at his side. Angelica swallowed hard.

"I guess that means I raised you right." Her grandfather sat back in his chair, grinning. "There are so many crazy people in the world, so many people who would do anything for a dollar. I wanted to see if you would follow your heart. I'm glad you did.

"I raised you to think about the consequences of your actions, girl, and decide if you can accept those consequences. And I am glad to see that you do that, no matter what. If you continue to do that in life, you will be fine."

Angelica was confused, but she couldn't help smiling. He was a jokester, even in death.

"I know you're confused." Her grandfather grinned at her some more. "And the answer is yes, I still leave everything to you. Lieberman will give you all the details. He will work with you until you are twenty-five, so you're not overwhelmed. Just follow your heart. All I ever wanted for you to be was a good person. I hope I succeeded in that."

Angelica watched as Pop-pop got up from the chair and left the room. The screen went black. Angelica sat silently. She couldn't believe it.

Lieberman broke the silence. "You all right? Would you like something to drink?"

"So it was a test?" she asked.

Lieberman smiled again. "Yes. Did you expect any different?"

"No, I guess I didn't. But what is on the other tape? The one I didn't see? What would happen if I—"

"Now that doesn't matter, does it?"

Angelica stood up. "No, I guess it doesn't. What's next?"

"What's next is you have a lot of paperwork to sign. Your grandfather set up several trust funds, which I will explain to you. We will have series of meetings so you can get the full grasp of your grandfather's—now your—holdings."

Angelica glanced at her watch. "Can we start later? I have a lunch date." She couldn't wait to tell Juan. He was not going to believe it.

"We can start tomorrow. Will that work for you?"

She nodded.

"What are you going to do now? And please don't say go to Disneyworld." Lieberman laughed.

Angelica shrugged. "Before or after I go out and put on my purple dress?" Lieberman looked at her, confused. She smiled. "I am going to take some time to think. Apply to music school. Think about where I want to live." She extended her hand, and Lieberman shook it with more enthusiasm than Angelica thought he was capable of. He walked her to the reception area.

"Just watch out for relatives falling out of the woodwork."

Angelica spun around and thought for a split second that not only was Lieberman smiling, he was grinning, too.

"You knew about that?"

"Of course, who doesn't? Nothing that exciting ever happens around here. It's been all over the papers. When Deborah first arrived, your grandfather had us investigate her. I was more than his estate lawyer, you know."

"I thought he was angry at Pastor Davis."

"He was. But they had been friends forever. He was mad at him for trying to find a wife on the Internet. He didn't think it was a good idea. And he didn't approve of his May-December preference. It didn't look good, especially for a minister. We even knew that she was involved in a marriage scheme. We had an eye on her."

"I thought he just didn't like her."

"Well, that, too. But your grandfather was very careful. Years ago, someone contacted him claiming paternity but then disappeared. We still think it was Deborah."

"What's going to happen to her now?" Angelica said.

"She is going to be very comfortable spending some time at the Mid-City Behavioral Health Center. You take care."

Angelica left the office, shaking her head in disbelief. Pop-pop had known about Deborah all along. She might as well get used to it. The world was full of crazies. She had no idea that she would be the star of her own soap opera!

She glanced at her watch again, and quickened her step. She was going to get rid of Jeanette and meet Juan for lunch. A smile came to her lips. They'd agreed that they would go slow and not do anything too hasty. The past week had taught her a lot of things, patience among them. Angelica was sure that good things came to those who waited. That, and she learned that every action, no matter how small, had a consequence. Who knew what it was that led Deborah's mother to believe Pop-pop was in love with her? That little thing was still affecting people decades later.

People seemed to be willing to do anything for the love of money. It was a powerful force. Above all, Angelica learned that, for her, no matter how good things felt at the moment, the best way to approach life was with common sense and self-love. When all was said and done, those two things were free.

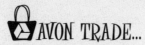

AVON TRADE...

because every great bag deserves a great book!